A Horse of a Different Color
T. S. Dawson

Acknowledgements

Thank you so much to each and every single one of you for continuing to give your time to my writing. If it wasn't for your encouragement, I would not still be pursuing this dream of my, of becoming a successful author. For that I owe you the sincerest of appreciation. Thank you.

Thank you to Wesley and Terry, my son and husband, for all of your love and support. I am so happy that you all are on this journey with me.

To the T.S. Dawson team, Donna Goss, Christie Hartley Johnson, John Bryan and Annette Saunders, thank you so much for all of your help. I really could not do this without your editing, critique and computer skills and for being my sounding boards.

Thank you for helping me to bring these characters to life and for keeping me motivated.

Thank you to the stores that carry my books, Genuine Georgia in Greensboro, Georgia, The Bookworm in Louisville, Georgia, The Paisley Bag in Wrens, Georgia and The Georgia College and State University Bookstore.

Thank you to Amanda Morgan Greene and Gay Hattaway Morgan for all that you do to support my writing and my efforts. Thank you for arranging for me to do a book signing at my alma mater.

Thank you to the ladies at SWW, you know who you are, who continue get me through the day job.

Lastly, thank you to my fellow Indie writers. Your advice, example and tenacity inspires me.

Thank you all from the bottom of my heart and please enjoy my latest work and tell your friends.

Sincerely,

T.S. Dawson

Prologue

August 16, 1996

Green,

    I couldn't leave without letting you know that I forgive you. I forgave you because I'd forgive you anything.

    In the beginning I was so upset with you. It was a wicked thing you did to Whitney Knox. I would expect something like that from her, but not from you. That left me wondering if I knew you at all. I doubted that the girl I fell in love with even existed. It wasn't until a conversation with your father that made me understand you were always the same. He asked me what I would do if someone messed with my sister. It made me take a long look at myself because as we know someone did do something and I did nothing.

    Your father said his philosophy was, "You can mess with me all you want, but you better not mess with anyone I love." He also said that he suspected you had the same philosophy.

    Although I don't condone that you only broke her arm and missed breaking her neck due to sheer luck, I do admire that you had the guts to stand up for the ones you love. Perhaps if I had done the same for mine and taught Dwayne a lesson when he hurt her, maybe he wouldn't have had the nerve to put his hands on you. For that, I owe you a sincere apology. I'm so sorry Lucy.

I must also apologize for not telling you this sooner and hope you can forgive me. I've always been better with horses and hounds than I have with girls, but with you things were different. You made everything easier and better. Even when keeping my distance, I looked forward to seeing your face every single day and I miss you more than you know. You're the first thing I think of in the morning and the last thing I think of at night. From the moment I met you, I could hardly keep my eyes off of you. You'll probably always be forbidden fruit, but it doesn't mean I don't miss your taste and the way you feel on my lips. Maybe I'm a coward because I'm just now working up the courage to tell you these things and maybe I'm a coward because the only way I can tell you how I truly feel about you is by putting pen to paper. For so many reasons you deserve better and I hope you find it. I hope you find all the happiness you deserve.

Love Always,

Edward

Chapter 1

December 7, 1996. Battle of the Bands.

Some of it was just noise.   Some of it was screeching, like someone pulling cats' tails. I thought my ears were going to bleed.   Others weren't bad. Then, there was a real stand out. They sounded like Pearl Jam and I thought of Lucy. In a sea of people, I thought of her.

We were packed in, body on body. The Battle of the Bands was the biggest event held at my college. The estimate was that forty thousand students from colleges all across the state trekked in for the event. The grunge, the preps, the nerds, the kids who you'd never think would be caught dead listening to any of this kind of alt music, all races, all kinds of students were there.

Among those in the sea of people that washed over the field of my college's football stadium with me was my sister Anne. She was set to start college here in the coming fall. Anne was two years younger than me and a year older than Lucy.

I sized up Anne as she bounced with the music, with the excitement of being at a real college party, her first college party, she seemed in her element.   Seeing the smile on Anne's face made enduring this spectacle worth it.   I liked music as much as the next person, but this wasn't my thing.

It was a pretty good light show for amateurs. There were flashes, hundreds of cameras going off, and beams of rainbow like colors that shot far into the night sky. Rainbows contradicted most of the angst filled music, but it kept up with the beat pretty good. The only thing that fit was the periods of darkness.

Anne stood right next to me, and through the blinding light and the pitch black in between, I could feel Anne's shoulder and elbow right through the sleeve of that barn jacket she wore. There was an ebb and flow to the sea that pushed her into me, me into the guy next to me and so on and then back again.

I don't like crowds. I don't like people shoving me. I don't like the smell of weed. I was out of my element, but Anne was right at home. She knew more of the music than I did. In fact, the only music I really recognized was the Pearl Jam songs and those songs made me long to talk to Lucy.

Who in their right mind went to a concert and wished they were somewhere else? I did. I wished I was with her, someplace quiet. I hadn't seen Lucy since the day I left Thomson to return to college. I'd called a couple of times, but a few conversations with her weren't enough. I tried to write her off. I figured it was better if she got on with her life. Lucy was only sixteen and I just turned twenty. She still had a year and a half of high school and I was three states away. These are the things I thought about constantly even now when I was supposed to be showing my little sister college life. Even the walk to the concert was about Lucy.

"You think about her all the time don't you?" Anne asked as we walked from my apartment to the stadium. It was a brisk night and I could see her breath when she spoke.

Anne was the only person in my family that noticed a change in me when I came home after my summer in Thomson, Georgia. She's the only one I told about Lucy and no detail was spared.

"Yeah," I confessed.

"I didn't think guys were like this."

Anne bounced in front of me and turned. She walked backward with her hands in her pockets when the conversation progressed.

"I like to think I'm not just the average guy." I winked at her.

"You're gonna marry her one day, aren't you?"

"If I'm lucky." I said it without thinking. I'd never really thought so far ahead as to think of marriage, but the thought popped out of my mouth and there it was.

"It's funny. Your sister wanted you to marry her sister. I guess I'll end up related to Lily one way or another." Anne had made friends with Lucy's sister, Lily, the summer before when she worked at the Wrightsboro Hunt.

"I couldn't tell you the last time I heard from Lily. I'm going to have to remember to call her when I get home," Anne nodded.

I would have settled with small talk, "How's your grades," and what not. Small talk wasn't Anne's thing. She asked the tough questions that made people think. Tonight's topic was Lucy and it made me think long past the walk to the concert.

The next wave passed through the crowd. This time the pushing came from behind us. A girl lost her footing, a girl that was smoking, and I took a sting from the butt of her cigarette as she started down. Unlike Anne, I didn't dare wear a jacket so the burn was straight to my skin. I stumbled a little as

9

well. Anne steadied me, but never took her eyes off of the stage. Once the wave passed, I checked the damage to my arm. I could hardly see it, but when the lights hit us again I got a look. A little blood and some singed arm hair was all there was. It was nothing I couldn't shake off.

Paranoia forced me to check to make sure my wallet and phone were still in my back pockets. I felt for them and they were in place. I sprang for my first cell phone yesterday and it was one of those flip jobs and it was tiny. Anne was as certain as I was that I was going to lose it.

"Hey," I shouted to get Anne's attention. "I'm going to go to the bathroom. Are you okay to stay here?"

I couldn't hear her reply. The strain on her face indicated that she was screaming. I knew what she said only by reading her lips. "Yeah, I'll be fine."

I gave her the okay sign with my fingers and did my best sign language to tell her to stay right there.

Although I had to use the bathroom, I really used that as excuse to slip away and call you. I weaved through the crowd and found the Port-o-lets lining the goal line at the opposite end of the football field from the stage. I passed by those and opted for the stationary rooms on the second level of the stadium. I wanted to get away from the noise to call Lucy and there was a balcony that circled the second floor. That would be the perfect spot to make the call.

I programmed the number in yesterday after I picked up the phone, but this was the first call I made. I flipped open the phone and scrolled through the contacts until I found, "Green."

I hit send and listened as it rang. The phone rang so many times that I began to expect that you were out doing what normal teenagers did on Friday nights, dating. The thought of that really ate at me. I was just about to hang up when you answered. I counted myself lucky to get you and not your mother or sister. I had had the same luck the other two times I'd called you.

"Hello?"

I slumped over the railing of the balcony, propping up with one of my elbows. "Hi."

"Edward?"

"Green."

"It is you!"

"I would say, 'In the flesh,' but..." But then I couldn't say anything because she laughed.

I loved hearing Lucy laugh. I loved having the ability to make her laugh. I'd never possessed the ability to do that to anyone before, well, anyone but Anne. Lucy's laugh was the best music of the entire night.

"I'm glad you think I'm funny." I smiled and wondered if she could hear it in my voice.

"Why are you calling tonight?" she asked.

"I'm at a concert and the music reminded me of you." I turned around and leaned back against the railing. I held out my phone for a second. "Can you hear that? They're playing Pearl Jam. I know how you like them."

"Which song is it?"

"Alive."

"Ah, I like that one, but my favorite's 'Black'."

Last summer, when I met Lucy Meeks, when we snuck around, she made me play that song every single time we got in my truck. Most of the time, listening to the same song over and over again would have driven me crazy, but now I find myself listening to it all the time just to remember how the wind blew through the curls on her head when she sat beside me and how the sunlight made her glow. I never asked her why she loved that song best until now.

She took a moment before answering, like she was trying to find the right words. "Because it was playing the first time I saw you."

The right words turned out to be more like a confession and it puzzled me. "But we met at the kennel and I don't remember..."

"Right," she said with a sweet sigh, the kind that called me silly without saying the word. "But, I first saw you the Friday night before. You were stopped at a red light in front of the movie theater. I was waiting on the curb for my mother to come get me. I've been a Pearl Jam fan ever since."

Now I was the one laughing. I got a hold of myself and said with all sincerity, "I wish you were here."

"I wish I was there, too."

I could hear the smile in her voice and in my head I could picture her. She was the prettiest girl I'd ever seen. All last summer, she was a magnet for me.

The muffled music stopped and thundering applause shook the stadium. "They're changing sets. I've got to go, but here, let me give you my number. I got my first cell phone today."

"Nice."

I gave her my number quickly with the intention of wrapping up the call. I had to get back to Anne. What kind of brother would I be, asking her to come for the weekend and then leaving her to fend for herself?

"Call me again, soon? Sooner than two months next time."

"Sooner than two months, I promise. And, you know, you could call me."

Lucy laughed.

As I did with each of my calls, I resisted the urge to tell her I loved her. None the less, it was on the tip of my tongue. I like to think she resisted the urge to tell me as well. I'd told her once, but only in a letter. She'd never told me, but I felt it. I felt to my bones that Lucy Meeks, my Green, loved me as much as I loved her. I didn't know what to do with that information as I tried to set her free, but just as I'd been pulled to her that summer I was pulled to her now. A thousand miles between us and she still had that power over me.

"Good night, Green."

"Good night, Edward."

I closed the phone, closed my eyes, took a deep breath and relived a kiss with Green. Lucy was so inexperienced with everything horse and hound related when she started at the hunt club last year that when I was hired by her father to give her riding lessons, I nicknamed her "Green." It is the term used to describe a young or unbroken horse and that is exactly what Lucy is, unbroken.

A breeze in the cool air floated across my face like her graceful touch. I exhaled and left to find Anne.

The light show from the stage was off while the next band set up, but a few of the flood lights on the side of the stadium allowed just enough visibility for me to see where I was going. I found the fifty yard line and one "excuse me" after another and one slosh of beer after another accidentally tossed on me, I found the girl with the cigarette who'd burned me earlier. Anne should have been near.

I passed completely across the field and back and no Anne. I found the girl with the cigarette again and managed to get her attention. I asked her if she noticed Anne and it was useless. She was drunk and slurring her words.

"Did you see which way she went, the blond haired girl that was right next to you?"

I might as well have been Dorothy asking the Scarecrow which way to Oz because Drunkness pointed in one direction with the cig, and over that arm, she pointed with her Solo cup of beer toward the other.

I had no idea where Anne had gone. Maybe she just went to the bathroom. The Port-o-lets in the end zone, I remembered. Just in case she was on her way back, I cut down the side of the field that we came in on. I scanned every face I passed and every face in the crowd on both sides of me. There was no sign of Anne on the sidelines or in any of the lines for the toilets. I waited and checked every face that opened a door to leave one of those ripe smelling things.

The next band was taking the stage and the rainbows hit the tops of heads across the field. A blaring rendition of Poison's "Talk Dirty to Me." Between the music and the screams, I was derailed.

The only thing I could think to do was go back to where we were and hope she was there. That didn't mean I didn't search for her all the way back.

I found Drunkess again, but no Anne. I ran my hands through my hair holding my head as I spun in all directions looking for her.

It had been an hour since I hung up with Green. I'd been searching and nothing. There was no trace of my sister. I didn't know what to do. I didn't know where to look. I was lost. Utterly lost, but worse was that I'd lost my sister. I waited ten more minutes, spinning in that spot, grasping for any glimpse of her. The pit of my stomach churned. I was nauseous. Nauseous!

"Dear God, where is she?" I begged as every nervous twitch I had manifested itself. I ran my hands through my hair. I rubbed my hands over my mouth until the point I was nearly chapped. My eyes flashed in every direction. Panicked and nauseous.

Anne would have done the same thing I did. If she had lost me, she would have come back to the last spot she saw me. She would have returned to the spot on the fifty yard line and she would have waited, but she wasn't here and she wasn't waiting. I was. I was here and I was waiting for her and the minutes ticked by, but the feeling of something being wrong wasn't easing up.

The music raged on, but the battle was within me. Did I leave that spot? Give up on her coming back and go get help or did I continue to wait for her? What if she came back and I wasn't there?

The answer came with gripping terror and it took hold of me. The wave of people washed around me, but I was now in a sea of people alone with the thought, Anne wasn't coming back. I had never been more alone.

Salmon don't run. They don't sprint. Despite that, I was the salmon going upstream against that wave and I was doing it at a breakneck pace. I edged past people as best I could. I shoved others out of the way. I yelled, "Excuse me," and kept going. I ran until I found a security officer. I blubbered my way through what was wrong.

"Call home and see if she's checked in," the officer advised. "If she can't find you, she might have called there."

It seemed logical, but I would rather have died than called and worried my parents. It was after 11:00 p.m. and my parents would be in bed. The phone rang once and my mother snatched it off the receiver.

"Mama, it's me," I tried to sound calm as not to alarm her.

Mama yawned, "Edward?"

"Yes, ma'am. Has Anne called home?"

"No, Edward. Isn't she with you?"

I could hear my father in the background, "What's wrong, Liz?" Her name was Elizabeth, but he called her Liz all of my life. No one else called her that.

Mama's voice was muffled. I'm sure she covered the phone with her hand, but I could make out what she said. "It's Edward and he wants to know if Anne's called here."

The next thing I knew, my father was on the phone. "Where's Anne?!"

I took a hard swallow before answering. "I don't know."

"What do you mean, you don't know?" My father was a demanding man and he and I'd butted heads for as long as I could remember. Stern and no nonsense, that was him.

"I left her to go to the restroom and to make a call."

"You left to make a call? Did I hear you right, son? You left your sister to make a call? Must have been some call!" He berated me.

The officer pacing behind me could hear every single word. I was no short man, but this fellow towered over me. He snatched the phone out of my hand and shook his head.

"Sir, this is Captain J.J. Wasden of the campus police. I believe I've got your son here and he seems to have lost his sister. Now, if you would kindly tell us if you've heard from the girl I'd much appreciate it."

My father might have met his match in Captain Wasden. Any other night I would have enjoyed this confrontation.

As easily as the officer had heard my father speaking to me, I heard him speaking to the officer and he took a softer tone. "We haven't heard from her."

"Alright, if she calls home, I want you all to call me as soon as you hear from her."

Then the officer gave my father his number. When he hung up and handed my phone back to me, he radioed for other officers. Countless uniformed officers reported to him at once and six plain clothed officers. I provided them a description of Anne.

"Long sandy blond hair. Blue eyes. She's a girl that looks an awful lot like me, but shorter. She comes up to about here," I motioned to my collar bone. I was a whole head taller than Anne.

"She had on a tan barn jacket. Jeans. I can't remember her shirt. Jesus, I can't remember her shirt." I shook my head.

I added, pointing to my own eye brow, "She's got a scar on her right eye brow."

I finished the description and they fanned out to search for her. Even before the concert ended, they had set up stations at all of the exits to look for her.

The music died down and the stadium lights came up. The cops looked and I looked. The crowd dissipated and no one spotted her leaving.

When the stadium was finally empty, they searched the entire place, top to bottom and bottom to top and back again. Every nook and cranny was picked over, including those in the parking lots, and there was no trace of Anne. It was as if she'd never been there at all.

From the stadium, I was taken to the campus police station. I was passed off from Captain Wasden to others for questioning. While I was interviewed, they sent officers to my apartment to see if she'd gone there.

"She's got shoulder length sandy blonde hair. It's a little lighter than mine. It parts in the middle and she tucks it behind her ears." I repeated my description of Anne in a quiet room where they could fully hear me this time. I was questioned by a man, but a female officer took notes.

"She's about chest high on me so about five foot six maybe," I ran a hand under my chin to the top of my chest. "And, her eyes are exactly like mine, clear blue."

"Has she ever run off before?" the female interjected.

"No! And she hasn't run off now." That's when it really occurred to me. "Oh, dear God, someone's taken her! Oh, Jesus Christ!"

I doubled over.

"Are you alright, Mr. Stephens?" Officer Robinson, the one doing the bulk of the questioning, asked.

"No. No. I'm not alright. My sister's been taken. Oh, God, it's all my fault."

"How is it your fault?"

The room was closing in. "If I hadn't left her," I gasped.

"Left her?"

I fought the urge to vomit. "I went to the bathroom and she was supposed to wait right there for me. Right where we had been standing all night."

"How long were you gone?"

"About thirty minutes?"

"Gone thirty minutes to the bathroom while at a concert with your baby sister?"

"I made a call before I came back. Oh Lord, Lord help me, it's my fault."

"Who did you call?"

"My friend Lucy."

"Your girlfriend?"

"No, not exactly."

"Yes or no." That time he sounded impatient.

"No. We dated over the summer, but..."

"But what? You left your sister alone among forty thousand strangers to call your ex-girlfriend." Judgement dripped from his lips.

Chapter 2

I knew my history. I knew what day it was. I knew what happened on that day. It didn't take the television to tell me. I knew the speech, "A day that will live in infamy." Of course the speech was about the day in 1941 when the Japanese attacked Pearl Harbor. I was as patriotic as the next person, but that's not why the day would live in infamy. For me, it was because that day in 1996 is the day my sister Anne went missing.

I had two sisters. I was the oldest of the three of us, then Isabella and Anne. I was named after the kings of England to which we were very distantly related. Isabella and Anne were named after the Earl of Warwick's daughters, the one that was the earl during the time of the War of the Roses. The historical figures of Isabella and Anne were tragic. Isabella had a scoundrel of a husband, George, villain of the wars who was constantly scheming against Edward IV to take the throne. Anne, although she went on to be queen after the deaths of both Edward and George and through her second marriage to their brother Richard. Richard the Lion Heart, who had his scandals as well.

Isabella was the most like my father. Mother insisted on calling each of us by our given names, but he called her Queen B from the time she was able to talk and argue with him. It stuck. Except for my mother, we all called her B. She remained the only one of us to have a nick name.

As soon as B figured out going to college meant leaving home, that was her means of escape. She ran about as far and fast as she could. She graduated a year early from high school and we walked in the same procession at graduation. Folks who didn't know us thought we were twins when our names were called back to back. The only time B embraced her association with our father or the family was when she applied to the University of Manchester where my father went. It worked to her advantage as his attendance there made her a legacy.

Anne loved family. The farthest she'd been from home was a stint as the kennel hand at The Wrightsboro Hunt in Thomson, Georgia when she was sixteen. She went there to help in the kennel and give riding lessons for the summer, but that ended about as soon as it began. I thought it was just homesickness that caused her to hurry back, but that wasn't it. I knew now that Anne had been essentially assaulted by one of the other kennel hands. He was the same boy that attacked Lucy this past summer. Anne didn't talk about it so I'm not sure exactly how extreme the assault was. It was just something that no one discussed. Lucy fought him off, but now I wasn't so sure about Anne.

Now, sitting in the office of campus police being questioned regarding Anne's disappearance, it occurred to me that Anne was headed down a more tragic path than even her name sake. She's likely been raped and now kidnapped. A cold shiver rushed over me at the thought. I'd never been so scared in my entire life.

"She had on jeans. Everyone had on jeans." I shook my head. That was a stupid detail that would help no one.

I remembered the barn jacket. "She had on a jacket. It was a little big for her. It was tan with brown corduroy trim on the collar and the sleeves."

I still described the most generic girl ever. I racked my brain to think of anything that would make Anne stand out, but there was nothing. I thought for a moment and remembered telling the officers at the field about the scar on her eyebrow. I told the detectives about that too. "It's noticeable. The tiny hairs are missing, like a bald spot, right through the center of her eyebrow."

"How did she get the scar?" Again I could feel the judgement as if they thought I did something to her.

"She was a baby and fell into the hearth of the fireplace when she was learning to walk." It was that innocent. She did it to herself.

I also remembered another scar and told them about that, too. "She's got a scar on her right shoulder blade. It's the size of the palm of my hand. She fell in the pool when she was six, scraped the side as she went in and took a chunk out of her back. It went almost to the bone. That's not something the average person would see or know about her." I didn't dare allow myself to think it and I didn't truly realize what I'd done, but I'd give them information to identify her body, if the outcome of finding her wasn't favorable.

"Does she know anyone else in the area?" I probably would have noticed a million things about the officer asking the questions, but the only thing about him that caught my attention was that he kept scooting closer to me.

"No. I mean, she's met my roommate once or twice, but..."

"Does she have her own car?"

"She does, but we walked to the stadium together. Her car's at my apartment."

"Does she have any health issues that we should be aware of?"

"No, not that I know."

"Does she have a boyfriend?"

"Not that I'm aware of. I mean, I don't think so."

"Does she spend the night out with friends regularly?"

"I don't know."

"Has your sister ever snuck out of the house before?"

"I don't think so."

"But you don't know."

"Well, no. I'm up here and she still lives at home with my parents two hours away."

"When's the last time you fought with your sister?"

"Excuse me? I don't remember us fighting since we were children."

"Do you have any reason to harm your sister?"

"What?" I came out of my chair on that question. "NO! Why would you think that?"

The male in front of me charged to his feet as well and went nose to nose with me as best he could being a solid five inches shorter than I was. I looked to the female officer for an explanation, but got none. She sat chewing the end of her pen.

That's when I broke. "Please, just find my sister!" I cried.

I was terrified, but not for the accusations that had been slung my way, but for Anne. It was after 3:00 a.m. and there was no word on her.

"Please." I begged as I flopped back down in my chair and dropped my head in my hands. "Please find her."

The door burst open, two officers were holding my father back and he struggled past them. I was on my feet again and bracing against the back wall as he charged at me.

"How could you?!" His words barely made it past my ears when he landed the first blow.

I took a fist to my jaw. It wasn't the first. It wasn't the last. I covered my head and went down as he landed another. It took three officers and my mother to pull him off of me. The last time he hit me like that I decided I wouldn't let him do it again. I was bigger than he was, taller by a few inches and out-weighed him by fifteen pounds. Tonight, while Anne was missing, was not the time and this was not the place to claim my man card.

"You are a disappointment if ever there was one! You better hope they find her, boy!" My father yelled as they drug him from the room.

My mother stayed behind. She fell to her knees and embraced me. She held my head in her arms and she sobbed with me. It also wasn't the first time she'd comforted me after one of my father's beatings.

As much as B hated him, and as much as they went at it verbally, our father never laid a hand on her. Anne somehow flew under his radar and Mama was his prize. The women seemed off limits to his abuse, but I was always fair game. They were the Philly, the pony and the mare and I was just a horse of a different color.

My father used every excuse in the book to be able to lay hands on me. One of his favorites was that I needed toughening up. Another favorite was that I needed to take my medicine. It never mattered what excuse he gave, Mama made excuses for him and tonight was no different.

"He's just upset about Anne."

Mama might as well have added, "It's nothing personal," as that was the tone of her voice. Since it was my jaw that was hurting and my heart that was again broken by him, it was very personal for me. For that, I slinked out of her arms. I stood up and straightened my clothes. I wiped my eyes and rubbed at my jaw. It hurt, but I didn't utter a word of complaint. As much as I hated my father in that moment, I knew he had a point. I left Anne. If I had just stayed with her, none of us would be here now.

The official police arrived, the ones from Rockford, the town where the college was located. The new detective and the Chief of Police looked equally blood shot in the eyes and fresh from their beds. They saw through their weariness and witnessed my father's spectacle. It really painted a picture of our family. If Anne had just run off they'd understand why, but that simply wasn't the case.

This process of interrogation or detective work was not as it appeared on TV, at least not any of the shows I watched. There was no immediate plan for a press conference or any release of a statement to the press. They said Anne was too old and that was for small children. My mother was quite upset by that notion as Anne was her child, her baby. They didn't even alert any news outlets. The word would not be put out to the public to help us find my sister. It was as if the Rockford Police didn't care at all, but they cared about something.

"You mean to tell me you're not going to help us locate her?" My mother flew in their faces and demanded answers.

"Ma'am, please calm down." The chief was an older man, like Santa in a police uniform. His protruding belly was the only thing that kept my mother from eliminating all personal space between them.

"I will not calm down!" She went up on her toes and almost nose to nose with him even with me pulling her back.

"I hate to be the one to break it to you," the chief said dismissively as he took a few steps back, "but she'll turn up. You know how girls are these days. She'll come in tomorrow morning doing the walk of shame."

The detective didn't make a sound. The nod of his head said it all and it lent support to his superior.

The thickness of my mother's British accent came shining through when she raised her voice. "I beg your pardon!" My mother was too ladylike to know the term, "walk of shame," but she had an idea what he was implying about my sister.

The chief went on to spell it out for her. "What do you think would happen if I put out an APB every time some girl met a boy at a bar and went home with him? Well, I'd be the biggest baffoon around, ma'am."

That's when I took over. "My sister is not that kind of girl, I assure you."

The note taking female from earlier who was still watching from the corner rejoined the conversation. "What do you know about the kind of girl she is? You don't even know if she has a boyfriend or the last time you had a disagreement with her or if she stays out with friends."

I was outraged. "I know my sister's not that kind of girl!"

The other thing I knew was that this would not fly in Thomson, Georgia. As guilty as I felt about the call to Lucy right now, I couldn't help but think about the afternoon last summer when she disappeared. Lucy was only missing for a few hours and the police were on the hunt for her like fleas on a dog's back. The guilt overtook me before I would allow myself to think on Lucy too much.

For a moment I started to pray, please let them be right about my sister. Please let Anne be a real whore that went home with a stranger. Don't let her be a good girl who's life depended on these assholes to find her.

The chief of police halted all activity by the campus. The patrols that were dispatched were called back. The unit was waiting at my apartment was dismissed from their shift. The search for my sister was abandoned. His intent was to protect the image of the college.

The College of Thomas Jackson was a small private college in a suburb on the outskirts of Richmond. It was named for General "Stonewall" Jackson of the Confederate Army. It was the pride of the area, the heart of the little town of Rockford, but in recent years the views of the Confederacy was changing. Southern pride was being overcome by what was called "political correctness."

The school had a world class Pre-Med program and it was highly ranked among schools offering degrees in nursing. For those reasons there was no shortage of new students. Despite the academic success of the school, the symbolic and very tangible stone wall that outlined the campus and the portraits hung everywhere of its namesake made it more and more difficult to compete for donors with bigger and more politically acceptable colleges and universities. This was my second year of Pre-Med and ever since I'd started, I'd witnessed the changes. A scandal such as a missing blonde haired, blue eyed teenage girl from its campus might just be the thing that drove the school under if word got out.

At 5:00 a.m., after pleading and bickering and begging and our refusal to leave, they escorted my mother and me to the front exit. Sometime during the night my father had been taken to the Rockford police station where he was booked on assault charges for striking me. Any other time I would have thought he got what he deserved. I didn't feel that way this time. The predicament my father was in only compounded the devastation my mother felt. I held her in my arms as she cried on the steps of the campus police station.

Just as we turned to walk to my parents' car, I heard a deep voice behind me. "Hey, man, you find your sister?"

I looked back to find the guy to whom I first reported Anne missing. I recognized him from the football field, but it had been such a long night and for the life of me I could not recall his name. He was clearly leaving from his shift. His shirt was untucked and the top two buttons were undone with his tie hanging loosely around his neck. The name tag was no longer attached to his pocket and was likely the piece of plastic he was fidgeting with in his hand.

It was hard to get past the lump in my throat to answer. "No, no sign of her."

I put my arm around my mother and introduced her. "I'm Edward and this is my mother, Elizabeth Stephens."

The officer extended his hand, "I'm J.J. Wasden, captain with the college police." He took back his hand after the introduction and stuck them in his front pants pockets. "I thought since they called us back that she'd been found." He scratched at his bald head." Captain Wasden rocked back and forth on from his heels to his toes as the conversation went on.

"The Rockford police took over and shut everything down. They decided there's no case here yet."

"Lord have mercy," he let out with a shake of his head and roll of his lips.

"They're more worried about the school's reputation than finding my sister," reluctantly I acknowledged. The disappointment in the school I had loved until tonight stung.

He continued to shake his head and asked the both of us, "And y'all are sure she's missing? She wouldn't have left the concert on her own?"

The both of us answered in unison, "No, sir."

He took out a pen and tiny notepad from his pocket. "Forgive me ma'am, but what the hell do they think will happen to the reputation if they turn their heads to the possible abduction of a young girl?" He asked as he scribbled something on the pad.

"This is my number. Go home and make sure she's not there and then call me."

Chapter 3

I wasn't at the bottom of the ocean. I wasn't trapped in a submarine with air running out. I hadn't seen hundreds of my fellow Americans blown to bits. I hadn't experience those things, but my December 7th would definitely live in infamy as well.

I washed my face that morning and felt like I was drowning in my own tears. I did everything I could to focus on the task of finding Anne because when I let the dark thoughts of what might have happened or might be happening to her enter my mind, that's when I felt the oxygen leaving the room and the walls closing in.

Anne wasn't at my apartment when Mother and I arrived that December 8th, that dreadful continuation of the night before. I unlocked the door and held it open for Mom to enter. Her feet barely hit the parquet landing beyond the door when she let out the most blood curdling, gut wrenching scream. A bomb had gone off in our lives and torn out my mother's heart. We had no clue what had become of Anne, but my mother felt it.

"In my heart, my bones and my soul, I feel the loss."

She couldn't explain it more clearly and I begged her not to say such things and to keep faith, but Mama knew Anne wasn't coming back. She was certain Anne was dead. She was so blunt about it that between her scream and her insistence, I wanted to tear off my own ears not to hear her. I didn't know if she'd lost her mind and these were the ramblings of a woman who'd had a break with reality or if she really could feel Anne. Either way, I was petrified and guilt ridden. I kept going back to the thought, if I hadn't left her, if I hadn't made that call to Lucy.

My father was locked up. My mother passed out on my couch. I offered my bed, but she was asleep before I could finish my sentence. My sister, B, was blissfully ignorant at college in England so that left me. I couldn't sleep and I'd been instructed to call Captain Wasden if Anne hadn't turned up. I gave it until 8:00 a.m. before I took out the paper and dialed the number.

"Meet me in thirty minutes at the main gate for the stadium," he told me.

I showered, changed clothes and slapped on some after shave to give me that sting to make me feel more awake. I grabbed the only photo of Anne I could put my hands on. It was actually a picture of all three of us together the day B left for England. I left a note for my mother and headed out.

The stadium was clear across campus from my apartment, but I made it there in record time. I was operating on pure adrenaline and sprinted the whole way.

I found Captain Wasden pacing in front of the front gate, crossing back and forth in front of the six foot by four foot span of letters, CTJ for College of Thomas Jackson, that hung across the gate along with the face of the mascot, Little Sorrell, Stonewall Jackson's horse.

"So, no sign of your sister?"

"No, sir." I frowned.

"And no word from the Rockford police?"

I repeated the same answer.

"Well, we'll see what we can do about that."

The gate was closed, but it was unlocked and he gave it a shove, pushing it back so we could pass. We went in and it closed behind us. I followed him through the corridor that led to the field.

"I stopped the cleaning crews already," he motioned to a group of seven or eight individuals milling around with garbage bags and wearing gloves and coveralls.

We kept walking toward a man in a suit that was fixated on the ground as he walked a path along the fifty yard line. The closer we got the more I started to notice a resemblance.

"That's my brother." The captain smiled back at me. "He's with the FBI."

Formal introductions were made and I stuttered through my own name. Captain Wasden's brother was a big dude and that alone would have been intimidating, but the gold badge on his hip took it to another level. It also rattled my brain that the FBI was being brought in to look for my sister.

"Ordinarily, we'd leave this to the locals to begin with, but since you've managed to pull the ace from up your sleeve," he glanced at his brother, "I'll go ahead and get started on this." It was overcast so to see us he lowered his black Ray Bans.

"The truth is," he continued, "statistically, if they aren't found within the first eight hours..."

"I got it." I cut him off. I just couldn't bear for him to tell me she was likely dead. I'd heard that enough from my mother already.

"Is that a photo you've got tucked under your arm?" He reached out.

34

"Yes, sir."

I gave him the photo and he looked it over carefully. "I'm also going to need something with her scent on it and I need that pretty quickly."

"Will her hairbrush do or do you mean clothing?"

Anne's brush and the clothes she changed out of before we went to the concert were both at my place. "I'll bring you both."

"Both will be great. I've got dogs coming and some other friends. Can you have your parents back here in two hours?"

I had to explain about my father, but assured him I could have my mother there.

"I'll make some calls about your father," the captain offered.

"Thank you both so much for helping me. Most of all, thank you for helping Anne. I don't know what we were going to do."

"Hang in there son. I can't make any promises about finding her, but we're sure gonna try."

They sent me on my way and the two of them stayed behind. I got the impression they were about to pull out all of the stops and really get some movement going on finding Anne. That was the one ounce of anything close to happiness since I hung up the phone with Lucy.

I raced back across campus and gathered the items and rushed back. I was then sent to the Rockford police station to sign off on charges being dropped against my father.

They put the two of us in a room together at the police station while they prepared the paperwork.

"Look," I said to him, "we need to come to an understanding."

He rolled his eyes and looked away.

"I'm serious. If you expect me to sign off on dropping the charges and letting you out of here, then we need to come to an understanding that you will never lay hands on me again. If you come toward me, I'm going to take that as a sign of aggression and you are going to finally have a real problem on your hands. You will never put your hands on me again. You will never take out your frustrations on me again. Do I make myself clear?"

I'd never spoken to my father like that before, but I figured this was as safe a place as any to make my point.

"And what do you think you're going to do about it?"

"I'm six foot three and weigh one hundred and ninety pounds. I'm twenty-five years younger than you are and I can run an eight minute mile. What about you?" I said while sizing him up. "You're long in the tooth and not what you once were so do you really want to try me and find out?"

"Huhhh," he let out in a puff.

"I'll also warn you that if you do one thing out of line to upset my mother or get in the way of any attempts to find Anne, if I get one sniff of you making this about you, I'll take you to the woodshed. You get my meaning old man?"

"I get your meaning." He leaned across the table in my face. "You're some big shot on campus and feeling safe in this police station. Huh," he grunted, "you'll sign those papers and drop those charges."

"Oh, you didn't hear them when they explained I have two years to reconsider dropping the charges. You know what that means don't you?"

He just glared at me. He had the same blue flame eyes that Anne and I had.

"It means you better be on your very best behavior for the next two years or you'll find yourself right back here or worse."

My father turned up his nose like he smelled something and rolled his tongue across his teeth, clearing a bad taste. He knew he was had and he didn't like it. He especially didn't like it coming from me.

"Remember, this is about Anne. If it was up to me, I'd leave you here, but my poor mother can't take much more and you locked up in here isn't helping her."

I also found it interesting that he still hadn't asked about Mother or Anne. I was just about to give him a what for about that as well when the desk clerk walked in with the paperwork.

"I'll just need you to sign here," she pointed as she put the pages down on the table and offered me the pen.

I shot my father a look before taking the pen, "Do we have a deal?"

"Fine," he hissed through gritted teeth.

I held out my hand and made him shake on it. Only after he'd given his word and shook on it did I sign the papers.

"Edwin Stephens, you're free to go," the clerk told him.

I thanked her, but he didn't. I quickly pointed out that he needed to say thank you and he rolled his eyes. I caught him by the arm and pulled him close to me. "I don't think you understand. We might need these people to help find my sister, your daughter, so you need to be as nice as you can and, if you think you can't, then you better figure out how to fake it."

My father glanced back to the clerk, "Thank you, ma'am."

The minutes of the day ticked by like hours. I accomplished everything and nothing all at once. The contradiction was in that I arranged all or did all that Agent Wasden asked of me, but still there was no trace of Anne. I kept busy to keep from thinking too much about her.

I gave them her brush and a bag containing all that she had on when she arrived at my apartment the day before. I'd never touched my sister's underwear before, but I folded them and put them in the bag with her other clothes. I didn't know what good it would do, but I wrapped her toothbrush in Saran Wrap and put that in too. I figured when they found her, I'd buy her a new one.

I managed to pack all of these things while my mother was sleeping and my father was smoking cigarette after cigarette on the front stoop. He gave up smoking more than ten years ago, but no one could blame him for starting back today. I judged my father for a lot of things, but having a cigarette or two or a whole dang pack today was not one of those things. If I had a vice, I'd probably be neck deep in it myself just to take some of the edge off.

At 2:00 p.m. a statement was issued in front of the main gate of the stadium. One of the others brought on by Agent Wasden gave a background, telling why we were all there, and then my mother spoke. Agent Wasden conferred with one of his colleagues and they felt it best if Mother spoke for us.

While a team of dogs scoured the stadium and we witnessed the buzz from the corners of our eyes, my mother tearfully begged for my sister's safe return. She stammered through begging anyone who'd seen anything to please come forward as even the tiniest of details would make a difference.

My mother was a woman who never left the house without makeup. B was like her in that regard, Anne, not so much. Mama's hair was always in place and she never looked under a million bucks. Now, here in front of hordes of news crews, tear stained, blood shot eyes, not a trace of makeup, she hadn't bothered with her hair any more than to run a hand through it. She looked like Hell, but her priorities were spot on. Her priority was the same as mine and the same priority became that of every news station in the Richmond area as well as the greater Washington, D.C. area as that's who all was listening to her.

The time for the college to be worried about its reputation was at hand and so was that of the town of Rockford. Mama praised Captain Wasden of the campus police for bringing in the FBI. "If it wasn't for him, I don't know what we'd do. The Chief of Police from Rockford said my daughter had just gone home with some boy, some stranger she picked up at the concert, but I'm here to tell you that's not my Anne. Please don't dismiss us like he did. My daughter needs you to help us find her. We love her so much and we want her to come back home."

My mother held it together and only paused to wipe her eyes and choke back tears once.

When Mother finished speaking the media closed in on us with a swarm of questions. The light from the cameras was blinding to my already tired and blurry eyes. Agent Wasden whisked us away while his team took over. As we fled to my parents' waiting car, I could hear a soft female voice settling the crowd with a description of Anne.

"My associates are passing out photos to each of you," she began. "Anne Elizabeth Stephens is seventeen years old. She goes by the name Anne. She was last seen wearing..."

My mother put up a fight about us being sent back to my apartment to wait. "We could help search," she argued.

"You'll help more by staying out of the way today," we were informed by one of the other dark suits.

Another advised us that we should have someone manning my apartment and my parents' home and the phones at all times. For whatever reason they didn't mention ransom, but due to our only experience with kidnapping being from movies and T.V., that's where our minds went.

"You think whoever has her will call?" I asked.

My father said, "We don't have much..."

"But we'll pay anything!" My mother stepped to the front of us. "Have you heard something? Has there been a demand? We'll do whatever we need to do to get the money.

"I'm sorry, no, ma'am. It's just a precaution."

40

And just like that the light in my mother's eyes was extinguished again.

Back at my apartment my father insisted that he drive home and wait by the phone there.

"We can call someone for that." My mother was hardly finished with her statement before he grabbed what was left of the cigarettes and his keys and he was gone. To me this was completely in his character, but to her he was just "so distraught over Anne that he doesn't know what to do."

"Yeah and that's why he hits me, too." It was a cheap shot at an inappropriate time, I admit. Maybe if I wasn't distraught I would have thought better of my words and kept my mouth shut.

"Edward Daniel Stephens, your father loves all of his children!"

I just shrugged and grunted an implied, "Yeah, right."

Chapter 4

Even though the night of December 7, never seemed to end for me, daylight came and went. I wasn't the only one that was stuck. In the days since Anne disappeared our lives went to shit.

My entire family was investigated thoroughly. No stone was left unturned. They even knew about Lucy, right down to every second I'd spent on the phone with her the night Anne went missing and each time I spoke to Lucy in the months before. They knew her name, date of birth, hair color and eye color as well as I did. I teeter-tottered back and forth between regretting that I ever met Lucy and wishing I was with her. I hated myself for making that call more and more as the days drug on with no sign of Anne.

They watched each of us like hawks, all of us except B. Although my mother phoned her and told her what was going on, the decision was made that B would stay in England. They knew right where she was and they wanted to keep it that way. Of course B wanted to come home and, regardless of what directions were given to her, the only thing that kept her away was the lack of money to buy a plane ticket home. B was never close to us the way Anne and I were close, but she worried all the same. She called multiple times per day to check in and find out if there'd been any change.

For me, the constant watchful eye of the FBI and the media was a strain. I didn't have anything to hide, but I was portrayed as they boy that lost his sister. It came off like Anne was a toddler and I'd left her in a hot car or something. I felt guilty enough without being put under the microscope and ridiculed as a fool.

The one bright spot was that I wasn't a fool and that showed through my grades at college. I had all A's going into my final exams. That allowed me to exempt all but one of my tests. I made an A- on that one, but not because I earned it. My mind was elsewhere and the Scan-Tron sheet looked like I had made strands of Christmas tree lights down it.

Quite frankly, I was given an A- to keep me quiet. The school could not afford any more bad press from the boy whose sister went missing from a college function and they, along with the Rockford police, chalked it up to her being a whore. No, they didn't need any more bad publicity from me and, were it not for that, they'd probably have kicked me out of school for having brought in the FBI. I knew this because they'd already fired Captain Wasden from the campus police for helping me. No matter where I went or what I did, I would forever be the black eye on The College of Thomas Jackson's reputation. For that reason, I would not be returning to college the next semester.

My dream of being a doctor, and what I'd worked so hard for all my life, was put on the back burner, but my life wasn't the only one in that situation. There was always the fear of what had become of Anne and what was becoming of my parents.

My mother's Christmas present wasn't any new revelation about Anne, but it was new

43

knowledge about her husband. My parents were under the same scrutiny as anyone else. Unlike my father, I had nothing to hide. As it turned out my father had something big to hide and he'd been hiding it for a number of years. For Christmas that year, my mother was gifted with the knowledge that her husband had been running around. Indeed, he'd been carrying on an illicit affair right under her nose for years.

It was Wednesday, right before Christmas when the news was delivered. My parents had returned to Rockford to participate in another ground search. It was the third of such searches. A volunteer group working in conjunction with the FBI organized them. This time it was a search of some woods along I-95 near Emporia and there was a clear reason to be there, unlike the others that were just searches of land near the campus. This search was the result of the one trace of Anne that had been found in all that time. A truck driver who had stopped along the highway to take a whiz in the woods found the jacket she'd been wearing the night she disappeared. There were several significant things about finding her jacket. The first of which was that there was no blood or other bodily fluids found on it. That gave us reason to hope she hadn't been harmed, just taken.

It was freezing cold and my fingers lost feeling in them fifteen minutes into the search. Like every other grievance I'd had since I lost Anne that night, I kept it to myself. We walked for hours and by the end my lips were blue and my toes were also numb.

Through trees and briars and all the underbrush of the woods, we walked and we walked, shoulder to shoulder, searching the ground. Regardless of the lack of blood on the jacket, I knew we weren't necessarily looking for more articles of clothing. I knew what we were really searching for and I was terrified that we'd find it. There wasn't a step that I took that my knees didn't shake a little and not from the cold.

The search was fruitless, but not without drama. The bloodhounds hit on a scent. These particular bloodhounds were trained in sniffing out cadavers. The whole place went into a frenzy when the hounds started to sing. Normally a singing hound was music to my ears, but not this time. At the fox hunting club where my father was employed and where I'd grown up hunting, I learned early on that a singing hound had treed a fox. It had done its job and found what it was trained to find. The music of these mutts was like nails on a chalkboard. It hurt to listen and I stood still like a child covering my ears from the noise. Although I wasn't right next to my parents when walking in the search, from my vantage point I saw them when they broke away and ran for the direction of the scent. They were promptly grabbed and held back.

"What if they've found her? Oh, God, I didn't want to see her like that..." I wouldn't' let myself finish the thought.

I made my way toward them and I could see my father rethinking the notion for a closer look. My mother didn't have the same reservations as the two of us. It took two volunteers and my father to hold her back. She demanded to be allowed to pass, to see her daughter, but they held her tight.

As it turned out there was a cemetery back in the woods and that's what the dogs hit on. I'm not sure if anyone else was, but my mother and I were relieved. My father just wanted the entire ordeal to be over with one way or another. I think he's started to believe what Mama's said about her not being able to feel Anne anymore. Despite his talent working with horses and hounds, my father was not a patient man. Sadly for him, something did end that afternoon.

Agent Wasden asked to meet with us after the search. My mother offered him tea as he took a seat in the living room of my apartment where he'd insisted we meet.

"Thank you. I've just stopped by to give you an update on your daughter's case and ask you some questions." Mama handed him the glass.

Regardless of her English roots, Mama conformed to the way tea was served in the south, sweet, like humming bird feeder nectar without the red coloring.

Mama replied politely, "Certainly," and smiled sincerely.

Dad rolled his eyes and huffed under his breath, "More questions."

Agent Wasden allowed my father's remarks to roll off and glanced around, surveying the room. He sized up the boxes and the general disarray. "Going somewhere?"

"I'm leaving school." Saying it made me feel the open wound caused by the decision.

"Ah, I see." He said nothing further on the subject and returned his focus to my parents. He opened his briefcase and took out a Ziploc bag that contained a piece of notebook paper.

My parents looked at it with bewilderment.

"This was found in the pocket of the jacket." He turned it around for me to see. The page had handwriting on it, cursive, but legible.

"Eddie, you took something of mine and now I've taken something of yours. – D."

My mother was steady looking at my father. Of course she looked at him. I looked at him as well. My sister had been taken by someone that had an ax to grind with my father. That's what the letter led all of us to believe.

"Do either of you know anyone that would call themselves 'D'?" Agent Wasden was more astute than we were. He didn't just focus on my father. He directed his question to both of us. "Edwin?" First my father and then me, "Edward?"

My father answered first and emphatic, "No!"

I didn't have a chance to reply as his answer was so quickly challenged. "What about Diane Reneaux?"

"What about Diane Reneaux?" My father leapt to his feet, flabbergasted and indignant, but knowing he was caught. He had the look of a treed animal, knowing doom was imminent.

"Sit down." Agent Wasden growled.

Ever the picture of oblivious, my mother did not put two and two together.

"Edwin, what is the matter with you? Sit down." Mother was embarrassed by my father's fit, but still so cordial to him.

"Off handedly, she answered Agent Wasden. "We all know her. She's a member of the fox hunting club where my husband works."

The agent just glared at my father as the color drained from his face and he returned to his seat on my couch.

Diane Reneaux wasn't just any member of the fox hunting club. She was the master of the hounds' daughter. Her father was the one that brought my father here to manage the hunt when I was a child. I was so young I had barely started to talk and, unlike my parents, my accent faded and I sounded about as American as the locals.

Ever since we arrived at the hunt Master Reneaux treated my father like the son he never had. He doted on us and no one really thought much of it.

Ms. Diane was an only child and she'd never married or had children. If she was a man, she'd already have taken over as master of the hounds. As it stood, neither she nor my father could be the next master.

It was likely Agent Wasden knew as much about Ms. Reneaux as I did and more. While our heads were spinning over the mention of Ms. Reneaux, Agent Wasden cut to the chase. "We have reason to believe that Ms. Reneaux is involved in your daughter's disappearance. She's being arrested as we speak."

Both of my parents gasped at the same time, "Arrested?"

My mother stopped with the one word and covered her mouth with both hands. My father expounded upon his shock.

"Not Diane! She'd never. You must release her." He was on his feet again, pacing the room. When his hands weren't running over his face and through his hair, he was ringing them together. "I demand her release!"

The veins popped out in his neck and his forehead. The veins in his head were nearly masked by the heat coming off of him and the beads of sweat that had sprung up.

"You've arrested her?" He turned on his heel and questioned again. I'd seen that look from my father before and it always preceded a beating. I half expected him to charge at the agent.

"Indeed." Agent Wasden only moved to adjust his posture in the arm chair at the opposite end of the couch from me.

"What the Hell for? She had nothing to do with this!"

As my father seemed more concerned with Ms. Reanaux, my mother became hysterical. "What about Anne? Where's Anne?"

I moved to the seat vacated by my father in order to be close and comfort Mother.

"We don't know yet," Agent Wasden hung his head.

"But, Diane did something with her? You're sure?" she asked as she wiped away tears.

Again my father insisted, "Diane has nothing to do with this!"

That's when Agent Wasden popped back at him, "Doesn't she? Are you certain there's not some reason she'd want to hurt you?"

"I don't understand." Mama held tight to my hand.

"Ma'am, we believe the note left in the pocket of your daughter's jacket was directed toward your husband by Ms. Reneaux." It was gently put, but didn't completely answer the question.

My father fidgeted at the window, looking out, but not really looking, as Mother's head spun back and forth between the two men. "But why would she write such a thing?"

I continued to watch. If I could have stopped Mother, I would have, but there was no stopping her. She wanted answers about Anne and she was entitled to them.

"She's my friend," Mother sniffled. "What reason would she have to hurt us? To hurt Anne?"

"With all due respect, ma'am, you'd be surprised what scorned women will do."

"Scorned? Excuse me?" The words filled the air as a look came over my mother's face, the color from her already pale face drained. She turned to face my father and the question went unspoken, but it was there all the same.

"I'm so sorry, Liz." He rushed back to her, dropped to his knees and took her hands in his.

"Sorry for what?" I think she knew the answer, but needed to hear him say it. In all the times he'd been hateful to me, she'd never lost faith in him. He was always a good person to her, but now she was seeing him as he was; flawed and selfish.

The agent must have wondered how stupid my mother was that she really needed it spelled out.

"I've... Well, Diane and I... I don't know why, but..." He couldn't bring himself to fully throw himself on the sword.

Mother snatched her hands from his and was instantly repulsed. She drew back and before he knew what had hit him, she slapped him. Her palm and all five fingers were imprinted in red across his left cheek. He flinched, but didn't say a word. Tears welled in his eyes. I'd never seen my father cry before, not in all of this regarding Anne, but now I saw tears. Real tears. He dabbed at his eyes and my mother recoiled to the far back of the couch and pulled her knees up between them.

He reached for her but I cut him off. "Don't touch her."

"My daughter is missing! What have you done?!!!" She unleashed on him at the top of her lungs.

"Oh my God what did you do to her that she would take Anne?!!!" Mother lunged past me. She went at him as if she had claws for hands and both Agent Wasden and I leapt to pull her off of him. She got a couple of pretty good digs to his face before we got her off of him.

"I will kill you if that bitch has harmed my daughter! I will kill you both!" If she could have screamed with more force I don't know how.

"Mom, please," I begged her. "Settle down. This isn't helping."

As time passed the investigation of Diane Reneaux was nothing short of a full cavity search of her entire life. They might as well have turned her inside out and made her wear her bones on the outside. By the end of it, the FBI knew every lover she'd ever had, what she ate for dinner on any given night as far back as the dawn of time and what sort of student she was in primary school.

They questioned each member of the Leesburg fox hunting club at length, some for hours. No less than five members had their homes searched. Some were as open and forthcoming as a Dr. Seuss book while others were put out and saw this as a major offense. It made them bitter toward us and it was only by the grace of God that my father was able to hang on to his job and the same went for me.

"People have affairs every day, especially people who run in the circles of the Diane Reneauxs of the world," my father noted.

"Yes, and if things turn south they just find the next bed, horse trailer, sketchy motel on the outskirts of town or what have you. They don't kidnap their lover's child. Is that what you're trying to say?" With her words my mother took shots at both my father and his mistress.

That was the gist of a screaming match I overheard my parents have one night. It was just another of the many fights they'd had since his indiscretion was brought to light.

"Honestly!" My mother slammed down one of the copper pots from the rack onto the kitchen island with a deafening clang. "What makes you so special that you could drive a woman to this? I hate to break it to you, but the sex was never that great."

This fell into a category of more things I never needed to hear. Since Anne had been gone, the filing cabinet in my mind that held that category was filling up fast.

My father had been sleeping in a guest bedroom, but that night she threw his things out on the front lawn while he was in the shower. She even grabbed his pajamas that were on the bathroom counter waiting for him and tossed those out as well. Dripping wet and draped in nothing but a towel, he gathered what he could carry and went to the apartment above the hunt barn. It was little more than a storage closet compared to the apartment I stayed in at the Wrightsboro hunt.

The thing that the FBI came to understand about Diane Reneaux and my father was that she was the town tramp and he was the village idiot. Their theory that Diane was a woman scorned didn't pass the smell test. Diane was not a woman scorned. To be scorned, she would have had to have been spurned by my father and that hadn't happened. She would have also had to have cared about him and she didn't. The FBI discovered that Diane cared for my father about as much as she cared for the other three married men from the hunt with whom she was involved.

The saddest part of my father's affair with Diane was that he actually loved her. I thought he was incapable of the emotion, but I was wrong. He was foolish enough to be the one sad sack that read too much into her flirtations and a roll in the hay from time to time. He actually thought he was special. It was discovered that on at least two occasions in the last year he had made plans to leave us and run away with her. So, no, Diane Reneaux was most definitely not spurned by my father. She was something, and there was a very specific word to describe what she was, but scorned was not it.

A week after my father moved out a man in a dark suit showed up at our door. I thought it was another FBI agent come to tell us they'd found Anne or some version of that or give us some update. He was no agent for the FBI. He was an agent of Diane Reneaux sent to make a deal with my mother to make sure the word about the affair was never spoken in public. The man was an attorney and he came bearing a deed to our house made out to my mother in exchange for her silence. Despite the thorough investigation, it never was public knowledge that Diane was running around with four men at one time and she aimed to keep it that way. The only people that knew were the Feds, my mother, father and Diane and the only one that would talk was my mother.

My mother neither accepted or declined the paper so the attorney left it on the coffee table. It was me that persuaded her to take it. "You can sell it and leave this place once we find Anne."

"Maybe," was all she said in return.

Chapter 5

It wasn't on the anniversary of D-Day or VE Day or anything significant. It was just a day. Unfortunately, it was the day that the lights finally went off on December 7. It was March 23, 1997, and it was the day we learned what happened to my sister Anne.

The wind blew and I floated back and forth in the front porch swing. I had fifteen minutes left of my lunch break, fifteen minutes until I had to give another lesson to another bored housewife. In all honesty, I had no room to criticize anyone when it came to boredom with their lives.

After I left college I had no place else to go. It was too late to enroll anywhere else and my mother needed me so I went back home to the house I was raised in. It was a Cape Cod style house with a front porch that spanned the façade and three dormer windows across the top. It was a modest house on loan to us as one of my father's benefits for working with the hunt. Now, with the stroke of her pen, Diane Reneaux deeded the house to my mother as hush money for her affair with my father.

The sun was beating down on my face as I thought about all that had come about as a result of Anne's disappearance. It was warm and the flowers were starting to bloom. The scent of the roses, the knockouts planted along the base of the porch, was floating through the air. I was starting to adjust to this new life and this was the closest thing to peace I'd had since December.

I sat in the swing and looked out across the field. Horses were grazing and one reminded me of the one Lucy rode, a chestnut mare with white on the bridge of her nose. Since I returned from college, I'd taken up my old job at the hunt barn here in Leesburg. I was giving lessons again, cleaning tack and mucking stalls. All plans to become a doctor were lost with Anne.

I despised living here. I despised it before I left for college and I despised it more now. I was Edwin's son and I was only an extension of him, his shadow. I liked to think I was nothing like my father and that all that made me who I was came from my mother and her side of the family. I was taller than he was. His hair was dark and mine was lighter, like hers. He carried himself as if he was sure of everything and had been all of his life. I didn't walk like that at all. He said I walked like a pup that grew too fast. As much as I embraced being different from him, that's what made him despise me, so I thought. To everyone at the club, I was nothing more than the hired help's son. I had been hunting since I was old enough to sit in a saddle, but I would never be one of them.

It wasn't until I went to Thomson that I truly felt like my own person. Unlike those of my home hunt, the Wrightsboro Hunt members didn't treat me like I was only there to serve them. With every lift of my hand followed a "Thank you" by the members there. It was a nice change. It was nice to be noticed and appreciated. In fact, I was treated more like a foreign exchange student than the help.

Being back here, back in my role as an indentured servant, made me miss Thomson even more.

My mind drifted to my time at the Wrightsboro Hunt last summer and to Lucy. Unfortunately the good memories of her and the summer we had were marred by the one lapse in my judgement.

The search for Anne was about as active as a dry creek bed. It had been all the rage before Christmas, but it went cold and there were other cases that needed attention. It had been almost four months since that dreadful night. On one hand time stood still, but on the other it had passed in a flash. Everything about my life now was upside down and backward. All that I thought was true and solid was shattered. The loss of Anne was the solvent to the glue that held us together.

I was kicked back in the swing, floating with the breeze, and trying to free my mind from the constant reflection of the turn our lives had taken. While I relaxed on the porch, my mother was inside packing. As disinterested in the case as the authorities had become, my mother was ever vigilant. She was packing for a trip back to Rockford where it all began. Mother was going there to lobby the police not to give up, the very folks who had given up on Anne right from the start. The Rockford police had been the first to think Anne's case was a lost cause and my mother was the last.

The horses played in the field across from our house and occasionally a lone car passed along the road, but other than that, the grounds of the hunt club were still. Our house was a part of the compound with the barn, the kennel and the clubhouse. My father now lived in the apartment in the top of the barn, above the stables. He lived very temporary, much the same way I did when I was in the hunt barn at Thomson last summer.

Out of the silence, the phone rang. The muffled sound penetrated the walls of the house and I heard two distinct rounds. A moment later I heard a violent thud and the house shook. For the house to shake like that something big had fallen or someone had fallen. The vibration was followed by a scream the likes of someone having been ripped to shreds.

I jumped to my feet and dashed to find the source of the scream. I knew all along the source was my mother and I found her in a pile next to her bed. She was heaving with sobs across the floor.

"Mother!" I fell around her and cradled her in my arms. "Are you alright?"

She struggled to catch her breath and when she did she mumbled the words we'd all feared. "They've found..." There was struggle in her face and voice. She couldn't complete that part of her sentence. ".... and they're certain it's Anne."

I pushed past the lump in my throat that accompanied the rising tears. "No. No! It's not her! It's not!" I don't know what I was saying.

My mother and I held one another until my father burst in the room. "I heard a scream."

Before he could continue and ask what was the matter with us, the look on our faces gave away the answer.

"No!" He was in as much denial as I was.

It had been four months and this was a logical outcome. Logical, but not easily accepted. There wasn't a one of us who hadn't prayed every day that

Anne would return to us safe and sound. With her back we'd all forget about the last few months and get on with our lives. I think each of us had made a resolution of some sort, something we would do better or fix about ourselves if only she would come back.

My father fell to his knees and tried to pry my mother from my arms, but I didn't budge. He gave up easily and fell slumped against the bed.

I'm not sure how much time passed while the three of us sat grieving in that tiny space on the carpet between the wall and the bed in the master bedroom. My mother's clothes were strewn across the bed, half in the flopped open suitcase and half out. There was no need for her trip now.

My mother was the first to snap out of the spell. "I have to clean the house. There'll be people coming."

"How do they know?" I wiped my eyes. I was still focused on the shock of the news.

My mother stood up and dusted herself off. She ignored me.

"Liz," he called her name in an attempt to snap her out of the glassed over phase she was in. "What did they say? Do we need to..."

For a moment my mother returned to our reality. She cocked an eye toward my father and snarled the side of her nose. "You don't need to do anything."

Ever since the day she'd found out about Ms. Diane, that's the attitude Mother had taken with him. With every word, she held herself back from eating him alive.

Mother left the room. He took his chances and pursued her.

I sat there with my grief and wonder and listened. They hadn't made it to the top of the stairs when he asked, "What about identifying..."

She took a deep breath and spit it out. "There's nothing to identify!"

My insides revolted and I felt the egg salad sandwich I ate for lunch coming back. I dashed to their bathroom. I barely made it. Each time I heaved the words "nothing to identify" rang in my ears. If I wrote new meanings to the words in the dictionary my definition for the word devastation would be "nothing to identify."

For the next week my father met with FBI agents to gain every piece of information they would provide regarding what had happened to Anne. He was a man possessed. It was the most interest he's shown in the case and now it was too late.

During that same time, while we waited for what was left of her to be returned for a proper burial, my mother cleaned our house. She scrubbed walls, carpets, tubs, toilets, baseboards and inches of the place that had never seen a rag, soap or a broom. She was a woman set on a pointless task.

B flew in from London and joined the madness. I don't know what she did aside of sit on Anne's bed and cry. To tell the truth, as possessed as my parents were with their activities, I was aimless. The words "nothing to identify" continued to bounce around the inside of my brain. The words were like a coin tossed into one of those donating funnels. The kind where the coin just goes round and round and round until you finally give up hope that it's ever going to slide down the tiny hole and join the other donations. Would the words ever go down?

Chapter 6

It was a long drive between Leesburg, Virginia and Thomson, Georgia. I only had my thoughts to keep me company.

Despite her feelings, wanting to keep her remaining children close, my mother put aside her feelings and did what she felt was best for me. She didn't want B to return to college, but knew that it had to be done. Like with B, my mother put on a stiff upper lip and called Mr. Watson to make plans for me.

Last year it was my father that made the arrangements for my summer job in Thomson. This year he was as interested in helping me as the man in the moon. This year it was my mother that sucked it up and made the call. She was the one that made the arrangements for me to work at the Wrightsboro Hunt again.

While driving I reflected on the sacrifices my mother made and how she did it with grace. She mostly sacrificed for my father and I couldn't recall a single time when my father had sacrificed anything for anyone.

"I know it's short notice, but is there any way you could take on my son, Edward, again this year?" she asked Mr. Watson when she called his office.

I couldn't hear his end of the conversation, but my mother explained to him, "We've had a family tragedy and it would do him wonders to get a way for a while and to have a purpose."

My mother had developed a rapport with Mr. Watson as he was my host family while working at the hunt last summer. Within moments she'd traded on that rapport and arranged for me to leave for Thomson the following morning. Even now, passing through the North Carolina countryside, I struggled to stay on route.

Last night I said goodbye to the few friends I had in town and this morning I said goodbye to my mother. There was an understanding that before she left for England she would visit me in Thomson. I cherished the bright smile she put on her face as she put aside her urge to cry and beg me to stay.

Passing through Greensboro, North Carolina, I passed a truck that looked just like my father's. It made me think of him and how I hadn't said goodbye to him. Beyond the wave of my hand across the field at him this morning as I headed down the driveway, I didn't even let him know I was leaving. A wave was as much as I felt he deserved. I resolved myself to the fact that I would be alright if I never saw him again. He'd never given much to me in the way of love and support and, since he blamed me for Anne and everything else that had gone wrong in his life recently, he'd cut me off financially. He refused to pay for me to go back to college. Now what good purpose did he serve?

I reflected on the last words he'd said to me over two weeks ago. "You're as dead to me as your sister.

Those words stuck with me. He was a cruel man and, if for no other reason than getting away from him, my decision to leave was a good one. I would miss my mother and I'd always miss Anne, but

I wouldn't miss my father at all. If I never saw him again, I would be okay.

Passing through town after town, but I couldn't describe one thing about them. I made most of the drive on auto pilot. At some point I started to allow myself to play the memories of last summer. My hands were on the wheel and my foot was on the gas, but my mind was elsewhere with Lucy. My nose was in her hair. I could smell the jasmine in her shampoo. I could almost feel my lips on hers. It was our first kiss and for a time I was transported back under the Halfway House. The mist from the rain sent chill bumps down my neck the same as her kiss sent them down my leg. I'd never kissed anyone like that before. Passion coupled with restraint, knowing she was too young and off limits, it was torture. Every time I tried to resist the magnetic pull toward her it was torture. Even now it was torture.

It was 4:15 p.m., just over ten hours after I left Leesburg when I took the Thomson exit off of the interstate. The one set of directions Mr. Watson gave my mother was for me to come to his office when I got to town. Following those directions, I turned toward town and didn't stop until I was at the red light in front of the old Belk building. The department store closed a few years back, but to folks around town it would always be the Belk building. That's how things were in Thomson. The Winn Dixie building out by Mr. Watson's office was a church now, but it would always be known as the Winn Dixie. Change was slow going in Thomson and that's one of the reasons I liked it there.

While stopped at the red light I could see the marquis on the Thomson theater. The theater was not one of the megaplex types. It was one of the few from the bygone era that only showed two movies at a time. I remembered the last time I spoke to Lucy and how she mentioned she saw me for the first time while she was waiting on her mother to pick her up after a Friday night movie. I must have been stopped in line for this very light. It was funny to me that I never knew that story, but I could just picture her there on the curb waiting. Things had come so far since that night.

The light changed and I continued past the theater toward the railroad tracks. The streets on either side of the tracks would take me around toward the Watson house on Hill Street where Lucy lived now. There was no use looking, the road made a hard turn so I couldn't see the house even if I tried. As I bounced across the tracks, I looked anyway. I could see the curve, but that was it.

It was probably nerves more so than jolting over the tracks, but my stomach soured. It didn't help that I always winced up a little on Jackson Street especially between the tracks and the intersection of Hill Street. The street had four lanes, two in each direction and they were so narrow that I feared I was going to hit a telephone pole on one side or another car on the other. Clearly, a full sized Bronco was not the ideal car when they designed this stretch of road.

My timing for lights was bad. I got stuck at the one at Hill Street as well. I could almost see the old house that held Mr. Watson's office. It was past the daycare near the crest of the hill. I would be there momentarily and I would have to face the music and, at the very least, hear about Lucy soon.

The same old plaque was out front. It was the same brown brick building with the paint still chipping on the shutters. Mr. Watson said he was going to get the place painted last summer, but it was the same as it ever was. Just like everything else I passed by on my way there, Mr. Watson's law office hadn't changed a bit. That's what I thought until I walked in the door.

I hardly had the door cracked when a familiar voice squealed my name. A thin girl darted from behind the secretary's desk where Lucy's mother used to sit. Before I could place where I knew her from, she threw her arms around me and gushed over how glad she was to see me. She looked so different, but there were hints of who she was. The voice, the hair color and the height made me question, "Lily?"

"In the flesh! Oh my goodness, you remembered!" She was stoked. She let go of me, took two steps back and sized me up from head to toe.

I was completely dumbfounded over her appearance, but Lily was at no loss for words. She continued with the flattery. "You are exactly as I remembered you!"

What was I to say to that? Last year Lily had been the epitome of sickliness, frail, pale and so skinny. Last summer she was in such a condition that she had trouble balancing. Yes, I remembered exactly how she looked as well.

I could see a trace of the Lily I knew from last year. She moved a little quicker, but the balance issue wasn't completely gone. With every move, she kept a hand on either the desk, the wall or one of the chairs in the waiting room. It was subtle and people who didn't know her probably wouldn't think anything of it.

"You look great!" I probably shouldn't have said that. Last year Lily had a huge crush on me and I didn't want to encourage that to start up again.

I glanced away and saw her name plate on the desk as she thanked me for the compliment.

"So, you're working here now?"

"Yes. I took over when Mary got sick." Lily's voice never deviated from its chipper tone.

"Oh, no. Is she okay? What's wrong with her?" Her voice might not have changed, but mine was filed with concern. All I could think was how awful it would be that Lucy's parents had finally come together and now she was sick.

"Morning sickness." So off the cuff, Lily said it as if it was something I should have known.

"Ah..."

"Yeah, it's nothing to worry about. I mean, the doctors have put her on bed rest now, but it's, well, she's forty-four and having a baby."

I suppose from Lily's point of view, the point of view of someone who'd battled cancer all her life, having a baby was nothing. That was not my point of view. I was still quite stunned.

"Oh, snap!" Lily looked at her watch. "I've got to make it to the post office before it closes."

Lily was moving the entire time she was explaining. "Here," she offered me an envelope from the desk with one hand as she picked up the stack of mail with the other. "Daddy left you the keys to the apartment. They're in here."

I took the envelope and thanked her.

"Come by the house for dinner tonight." She grabbed her keys and started around again.

Lily having keys was something else new. Apparently she was driving now. I refrained from commenting on that, but answered her regarding the invitation to dinner. "Oh, umm... I really can't impose."

"It's no imposition. I invited you. Plus, you have to eat, right?"

"I really shouldn't."

I held the door open for Lily, but she stopped short.

"Look, if you're worried about Lucy, don't. You might as well know, she's been dating Wilson Knox for a couple of months."

I felt like I'd just been gut punched by the elephant in the room. I really hadn't seen that one coming.

Sitting in the living room of the apartment above the hunt barn that night, eating the McNugget meal from McDonalds, I wondered how that conversation with Lily ended. I clearly wasn't over there having dinner, but I couldn't recall if I thanked her for the invitation, declined again and went on my way or if I just had a "What the Hell?" look on my face as I stumbled back to my vehicle. I still felt that punch all the way to my backbone.

The ladies of the hunt had remodeled and redecorated the apartment during the winter months. The paint was fresh and the fumes filled the air. There were new faucets, two window unit air conditioners now instead of one and all new furniture. The bedframe and mattress were new, too, and that was a relief. The old mattress was lumpy and the rumor was that it had seen more action than a bed at a sleazy motel. Regardless of all of the updates including the bed, I hardly slept.

I tossed and turned all night. When I did manage to catch a few winks, I had nightmares. It was the same nightmare I'd been having for a while. I was standing in the middle of a field, planted with peas or cotton or something. Anne was in the wood line just out of sight. She was calling to me, "Edward!" She wanted me to come find her. Her screams started out like those of a child playing hide and seek, but they escalated to screams of terror, calling my name to save her. No matter how fast I ran or jumped the rows of whatever it was that was planted in the field, I just couldn't get to the woods.

When I woke up in a startled flinch, I was winded from running. It was as if it wasn't a dream at all. As soon as I came to my senses and figured out that it was in fact a dream, my first thought was of Lucy and Wilson Knox. Awake or asleep, I was tormented.

Lucy got her wish last year of wanting to live on Lee Street. It's where a lot of the Thomson old money resided. Now, if she really wanted to secure her spot among the elite, attaching herself to Wilson Knox was a good move. I didn't think she was hung up on social climbing, but what did I know? I hadn't spoken to her since December and my own actions gave a pretty clear indication that I had no claim on her. I spent the last half of the year before trying to set her free and the first half of this year ignoring her. Now that I had succeeded admirably in my efforts to make her move on, I was less than thrilled. I was physically ill over the thought of her with anyone else.

I wandered to the kitchen in the dark and fixed myself a glass of water. Looking out of the kitchen window I could see the full moon hanging in the sky directly above the kennel. I didn't know for sure, but I figured Lucy would be working at the kennel again this year. She would probably be out on the hunt with us at some point, too. I swallowed hard and wondered how long it would be before I had to face her. I wondered how she would react. I wondered if there was any chance of winning her back. Was I so petty that it took finding out she was with someone else to make me want her? I hadn't ever stopped wanting her, denying it had just been a part of the punishment I inflicted on myself for what I let happen to my sister. It always came back to the fact that if I hadn't called Lucy that night, I wouldn't have lost Anne.

I settled back into bed on my side. I fell back asleep with the image of Lucy lying face to face with me. Closing my eyes, I could almost feel her graze her nose lightly up mine. The few times Lucy initiated a kiss, she did that. She ran her nose over mine. It was light as a feather and the sensation was a cross between a tickle and a butterfly kiss. It never failed to give me chills.

I fell asleep knowing I wanted Lucy, but when I woke in the morning the guilt was back.

Chapter 7

Day one, the word was out that I was back. One after another I had lessons all day long. Although it had been news to me when Lucy told me, the ladies of the hunt loved me. Apparently they all had a crush on me which I found amusing. Anne teased me about being the ugly duckling, said I "grew into my good looks." Maybe they were right because I knew it sure wasn't my winning personality that kept the ladies booking my time. Either way, there wasn't a moment to look toward the kennel, let alone walk down there and say hello to Lucy.

Day two, Wednesday, it was hunt day and inevitable that I would run into Lucy. If she was working with the hounds she'd be there. If she wasn't working with the hounds, she'd be riding in the field. Master Pate had made a special trip to find me in the ring this morning while I was training Mrs. Harper. He invited me to ride with the whips again and I felt honored. I'd have been fine with any invitation to ride, maybe more so if he had left me to ride with the field. In the field I could have conquered my fear of seeing her.

The hounds caught the scent of a fox straight away and the chase was on. The breed of the fox dictated the direction he ran. One color made small circles and another made large circles. The dogs picked up on the scent and ran in the same circles, but in a pack.

I was paired with Mr. Harper, also a whip, and we were sent through the pasture and through the woods to the left of the hunt barn. Master Pate, the current master, took two other whips and they dashed after the hounds straight up the middle. Another group was sent to the right. The job of the whips was not only to look for the fox and follow the dogs if they ran in our direction, but also corral any strays. Sometimes a dog got distracted and ventured away on his own. We had to keep an eye out for those. We also had to keep the master apprised of our findings by way of the walkie-talkie. The field, the majority of the riders, lingered behind.

It was fast paced. The hounds circled and circled and we gave chase. The chase ended within spitting distance of I-20, approximately five miles from the hunt barn. Nothing got the blood pumping of the hunt members more than when they caught a fox and today they caught one.

Old Master Pate couldn't ride a horse anymore. He was every bit of eighty years old and he hadn't sat in a saddle in ten years as far as I'd been told. That didn't stop him from keeping up with the hunt. He drove that Ford F-150 of his through the woods like he was driving a stallion. The truck had the dings and scratches to prove it. On one occasion last year he knocked the passenger door clean off. He said he hit a sapling, but it was a two hundred year old oak.

That afternoon, Master Pate found his way back deep in the woods like he usually did. He was there with what they referred to as refreshments and served up the toast.

"Edward, my boy, you're almost twenty-one. Wha-da-ya have?" His shaky old voice offered from where he was standing next to the truck. I could hardly see him for all of the horses and riders swarming the truck getting their drinks.

There was a girl in the back of the truck mixing drinks from the tool box. She had a series of liquor bottles sitting on top of the right side of it. Of course Jack Daniels was among the bottles in the tool box along with his cousins; Jim Beam and both of the Johnny Walkers as well as their friends 7-up, Coke, Diet Coke, soda and ginger ale. I wasn't one for drinking, but I didn't want to be the judgmental outcast either so I gave my request. "Jack and Coke, if you've got it. Thanks."

I didn't give the girl a second look until she finished making my drink and turned around. Her hand shook a little as she offered me the red cup.

"Lucy, is that you?" I was caught off guard.

I hadn't recognized her from behind. Her hair was longer like she hadn't cut it all year. It fell past the middle of her back. What had been full of curls was weighed down and only had a gentle wave. She'd clearly been in the sun more because it was streaked with natural highlights.

The horse I was riding was temperamental. I had been struggling with it all day. At first I thought it's commands were backward, but that wasn't it. It was just stubborn as a mule. As I tried to contain my emotions and keep my thoughts from showing on my face, the horse continued to try to do the thinking for the both of us. As if I wasn't nervous enough, when I went for my drink the horse bucked and kicked at the one behind us. I lunged forward out of the saddle and, while reaching for the Jack and Coke, I knocked it out of Lucy's hand and it went all over her.

"Looks like I'm not the only one that's green out here." Lucy glared at me as she took a good swipe at the front of her shirt and tried to ring out the liquid.

"Way to go, son!" one of the men chuckled.

A roar of "Atta-boys!" and "Good jobs!" came from the other, more crude men who saw what happened.

Lucy had on a white t-shirt with the WH logo for the hunt on the pocket. The shirt was instantly transparent. Her face turned a million shades of red as all of the men tried to get a look. They were already swarming on their horses around the truck collecting their celebratory drinks, but now it wasn't the drinks they were after. They giggled. There wasn't anything more to see than her bra, but all of them had their eyes trained on her. I wanted to punch each and every one of them in the face. Fortunately, the numb-skull of a horse I was on stood still long enough for me to shimmy out of my hunt jacket to give it to her.

"Here." I extended the offer. "Take this." I circled to the tailgate holding it.

Lucy took the coat and put it on.

"Party pooper!" said the same man who'd made the earlier comment.

Lucy shot daggers at him.

"Whoa. I was just teasing." That ass was lucky her father had been called to court and couldn't make the hunt that afternoon.

Lucy said "Thank you," but her tone was that of "Eat shit and die." She rolled her eyes and started back to the tool box. I was doubly glad she took the jacket. It gave me the opportunity to get out of the thing before I melted. Hunt attire was not suited to the Georgia climate. It was every bit of ninety-five degrees outside.

Even mad, and she was visibly mad with me, Lucy was eye candy. She was eye candy more so this year than last. I would have never expected that to be possible, but it was. Just looking at her made that gut wrenching feeling of guilt dissipate.

While I restrained myself from lashing out at the so-called gentlemen of the hunt, I gripped the reins of the wild animal I was quite literally saddled with and pondered ways to get Lucy alone. At the same time, the members of the hunt that made up the field came trotting up. All of them circled the truck, placing their drink orders. To keep my mule from embarrassing me or anyone else further, I backed him away and he actually obliged. To the far edge of the group we went and I sat there stewing. From there I could see a new addition to the riders in the field.

I recognized the face, but I'd never seen him at the hunt before. I met him once last summer at the hospital with his sister. Lucy put his sister Whitney there when she sought her revenge, unhitched the under belly strap of Whitney's horse and had it throw her to the point that it only missed inches of slamming her into a tree and breaking her neck. Thinking more about my own situation with Anne now, I understood why Lucy did what she did. The two girls were arch enemies and I'd witnessed the scorn between them on more than one occasion, but Lucy didn't exact revenge on Whitney on her own account. She did it because Whitney hurt Lily, her sister. All of that being the case, I had been trying to wrap my mind around the match since Lily first told me that Lucy was seeing Wilson Knox. If I knew who hurt Anne, I couldn't imagine giving one second of my time to anyone related to them. Low and behold, neither Wilson Knox nor Lucy felt the same as me. There they were chumming it up and it really got at me.

I sized up my competition and, regardless of their family history, I could not imagine Lucy being attracted to that squirrel of a boy. Even atop his horse I could tell he was barely as tall as Lucy was and she was a whopping five foot four inches tall. He had blonde hair like his sister. I always assumed Whitney dyed her hair that color, but maybe I was wrong or maybe he dyed his too. I chuckled at the thought. His skin was pale and fair like hers, and almost as pretty. He hadn't made an impression on me the day at the hospital, but he did now. I tried not to stare, but the more I looked at him the more unbelievable I found the situation. He really was, for lack of a better word, pretty.

The most important thing about Lucy and Wilson's interaction was that she looked my way three separate times. Not for an instant did I believe the look was because they were talking about me. She looked of her own free will and that was a good thing. Each time I held her gaze until she either became visibly frustrated with me or until her attention was called back by him mentioning her by name. The fact that she looked my way gave me hope.

The hounds stirred about and I figured there was no time like the present to start gathering them. That's when I got the idea of how I would get Lucy alone.

"Another round?" Lucy was snapped back to her task by the shaking of the old master's ice in his cup.

Wilson moved his horse along after the old master gave it a swift slap on the ass.

"Scotch, right?" Lucy returned to the tool box.

"We're gonna make a bartender of you yet." He gave her a wink and, as she reached for his cup, he reached and took the whole bottle and turned it up.

There was a third of the bottle left when he took it from her, but only a fraction of that fraction was left when he turned it right side up again. Lucy's eyes grew wide and so did mine, both of us knowing the same thing. Lucy was expected to ride back with him. I couldn't let that happen. I fell right back into the role of her protector.

"Master Pate, you think you can get back without Lucy? I could stand to have her head on back to the barn with me and help round up the hounds before dinner."

Dalton Pate, Jr., was the old master and his son, Dalton Pate, III, was the current master. Although I was certain number three was the one that arranged Lucy's transportation today, he wouldn't dare embarrass his father by pointing out that he wasn't allowed to drive unaccompanied through the woods anymore. Old Master Pate released Lucy to me as his priority had always been the care of the hounds, that's what I'd been told anyway.

Lucy didn't speak up and give her opinion one way or another. She just looked at me, turned up her nose and shook her head.

Old Master Pate answered for himself and gave me permission to take her. I held my mule beside the truck while Lucy made sure things were back the way she found them in the tool box and closed the lid. My stomach did flips as I watched her. She was wearing shorts and when she bent over in the tool box, I could see the curve of her ass where it met her leg. I had to look away for fear of drooling.

It felt so good to have her arms around me even if it was just for hanging on for the ride. I directed the horse back through the woods toward the hunt barn. There was a path, but not much of one.

At first it was at a break neck pace with my heart beating as fast as the horse's hooves. I let the horse run for a good distance, but once we were far enough away from the field and the pack of hounds that I could no longer hear them I slowed the horse.

"You ever seen the rock wall before?" I looked over my shoulder and asked her.

I could feel her shake her head, but I didn't dare keep my eyes on her long enough to see the answer.

"I can feel you do that, but you know I can't see you shake your head." I tried to make her laugh, but it didn't work.

When we came to the rock wall, an area where a creek had been dammed up in the 1800's with a fifteen foot high stacked stone wall, I gave a suck of my teeth and a "Whoa" to the horse. I remembered to tug the opposite direction of which way I actually wanted the horse to go. I gave the left reign a gentle pull and, like I had come to expect, the horse sent right. He walked over to the bottom of the waterfall made by the creek flowing over the dam. The trees hung over and made such a shade that it felt like spring and not the heat of June. This was the most beautiful place in all of the property to which the hunt club had access. It seemed like there wasn't a soul for miles but us and the only sound was that of the babbling stream. Picturesque is what it was. It was the perfect place to kiss Lucy, but I knew this wasn't the right time.

I eased down from the saddle and then offered her a hand. It was like she just fell into me. Again, I had to focus on something other than her face or I'm not sure I could have kept from throwing myself at her.

To keep my head on straight, I escorted the horse to the watering hole while Lucy wandered over for a closer look at the waterfall. She stepped from one stone in the creek to the next. I could see she was being careful of the slick moss growing on some and the slipperiness from years of water spraying on others.

I watched, paying more attention to her than the horse. Lucy didn't slip. She made it all the way to the largest rock in the middle of the stream, directly at the base of the falls. She was close enough that the spray coming off of the rocks showered her.

I didn't know what Lucy was thinking, but the anticipation of finding out was killing me. If she was going to yell at me or just tell me she hated me, I needed her to get it over with so we could move on. I needed her to tell me how she was feeling so I would know for sure what kind of shot I had. Now that I had her alone, I didn't know what to say and she hadn't spoken a word. I finally worked up the courage.

"How was school?" Of all of the meaty conversation we could have had, that's what I asked her.

"Fine." Short and to the point, she replied without a glance my way. I could barely hear her over the sound of the rushing water.

A few more stale questions with equally stale answers and then we started to get somewhere.

"How was prom? You did go, right?"

"Yes, I went. It was fun." I could tell she was holding back and that wasn't the full answer.

"Who did you go with? Anyone I know? I'm sure you had tons of offers." I tied the reigns loosely around a low hanging branch so the horse could continue to drink and I started in Lucy's direction.

"That really isn't any of your business." She took a sweet tone. If she was trying to taunt me, she was doing a good job.

"Wilson Knox?"

Silence followed. I jumped to the first rock in the stream and Lucy took a step farther away.

"How was college for you?" she asked, but, turning her back, she didn't appear to care about the answer.

I just wanted her to talk to me. More than that, I wanted her to kiss me under the spray from the water fall.

I wasn't ready to tell her about Anne, but I wasn't going to lie either. I wish she could have read my mind, known all that happened and how it affected me and how sorry I was that I let it affect her. For now, it would remain locked in my head and Lucy would stay at arm's distance or more. I hated being this close to her and this far away all at the same time.

"Come on. We better get going. We've got work to do." I hung my head and plodded back to get the horse.

Back at the hunt barn we went about our job of gathering the hounds and putting them up for the night. All of them came back with the pack except one and we found it fast enough using the tracker.

We ate dinner, not together. I ate with the other whips, all dying to know what was going on at the Virginia hunt, and Lucy ate with Lily and Mr. Watson. Lucy's mother was still on bedrest. Lily and Mr. Watson came to the hunt just to get out of the house and have dinner.

Wilson Knox sat with them. In fact, Wilson practically sat in Lucy's lap. It didn't seem to bother anyone. There was hardly a second since they met up in line before dinner that he wasn't touching her; rubbing shoulders, draping around her, just falling all over her. There was also the laughing, the high pitched laugh of his. It was unnerving and annoying. Lucy wasn't that funny, but he laughed, giggled almost, over everything she said. I couldn't hear it all, but honestly, he was like a gushing school girl.

Mr. Watson spoke to me and thanked me for loaning Lucy my coat. She told him what happened, but not about the cat calling. I'd kind of hoped she'd keep the coat. I liked the thought of her wearing it. It was the closest thing to a Letterman's jacket I owned.

Mr. Watson drove Lily home shortly after our conversation. Lucy stayed to help clean up and close the kennel. She was carrying leftover jugs of tea, two in each hand, to Mrs. Harper's minivan when I offered to help.

"Let me carry those for you." Her hands were full so I took the two jugs in my left hand.

"Thanks." She glanced at me and for a second I think she allowed herself a good look at me. I had a slight scruff of a beard on my face and I thought that made me look more like a man than the boy. I wondered if she liked me like this. I hadn't seen her look at Wilson Knox like she looked at me, head to toe, checking me out. That thought was comforting.

We were just about to Mrs. Harper's minivan and I came out with it. "Are you and Wilson Knox really an item?"

"An item?" For a moment Lucy slipped giving an indication that the thought of that was preposterous, but she recovered quickly. "You really have some nerve!"

Lucy stormed on toward Mrs. Harper's car and I followed. She threw open the back hatch and put what she was carrying inside.

"You know," she turned around and glared at me, "I don't need you to be nice to me. I stopped needing that around March when I finally accepted that you weren't really interested. So, just stop it! I'm not your summer fling this year."

I handed Lucy the jugs of tea and turned to leave. She said leave her alone. She clearly had something going on with Wilson Knox, whatever it was, so I did like she asked. I stopped it.

"Go ahead! That's just like you! Shut down and walk off!" Lucy yelled at me.

There wasn't much of anyone around to hear her, but the few that were around got an earful.

I whipped around, "Really? Is that what you think of me?"

"Coward!"

"Hot head!"

Lucy's mouth fell open. "What did you call me?"

"Hot head. You know, if you were so broken up over me not calling, you could have called me. You could have picked up the phone and found out if there was something going on. Was there something more important than the way I felt about you? And, you know how I felt about you! You could have bothered to try to find out what was going on with me and my family."

"Girls don't call boys."

If Lucy thought she had the upper hand, she was sorely mistaken. "Really, girls don't go around sabotaging other's saddles. You'll do bodily harm to someone, but you won't pick up the phone. Really, Lucy, really?" I left her standing there for the second time.

"I liked you better when you called me 'Green'!"

I threw up a hand and waved her off dismissively, "I liked you better when you were green."

I kept walking.

Chapter 8

That night my mother called. Talking to her was a nice change from the solitude.

"I think she hates me," I concluded after telling my mother all that had gone on with Lucy.

"There's a fine line between love and hate," Mother tried to console me.

I loved hearing her voice. There wasn't much left in the world that made me feel like I ever had a real home, but her voice was it. She'd maintained her British accent after all these years, but she'd taken on some American sayings and sentence structure.

As I dwelled on the fact that her accent never changed, Mama added, "I would know, I lived with your father for all of those years."

"I'd rather her not hate me."

"Well, hate is an emotion and at least it shows she feels something for you. If she didn't still care for you, she wouldn't be so mad."

I really hadn't looked at it like that. "So you think there's still a chance?"

"Of course. I think you just need to give her some time. Let her come to you."

That was the most advice I'd ever gotten on girls from anyone other than Anne. "Thanks, Mom. I miss you."

"I miss you too, Edward."

"Mama?"

"Yes?"

"I miss Anne."

"I know. I miss her too. Every single day."

There was a long pause. I would have been content to sit and listen to my mother breathe through the phone. Finally she broke the silence.

"I'm planning on leaving for England in a few weeks. I've sold the house back to Diane. You wouldn't believe how much she gave me."

"That's good. I mean, good that she bought it back from you and gave you a fair price, but..."

"Edward?"

"Yes, ma'am?"

"You know it's not your job to worry about me, right?"

"I know. It's just that I can't help it. It's what I do."

"I'll keep my promise. I'll come there and then you can take me to the airport in Atlanta. I'm kind of excited about it. Your Aunt Merty and Uncle John own a pub. I'm going to live above a pub in the town over from where I grew up. They might even have a job for me. "

"And you'll be near B. That's good for you, Mom."

That was a great relief to me. To know my mother was coming and I wouldn't be alone was nice, but knowing she was going to be near family and she wouldn't be alone was even better. She'd lost so much and I wasn't sure if she'd ever been truly happy before. I didn't want her to forget me or forget Anne, but I wanted her to move on with her life. She stood a better chance of that in England than she did in Virginia, across the driveway from my father's watchful eye. It had only been a couple of days since

I arrived back in Thomson, but it had been the loneliest of my life. I didn't want her to be lonely like me.

It seemed like forever passed before I saw Lucy again. She was cold and that coldness continued. She was strictly business. I couldn't get the image of her face out of my mind. She was gorgeous and the more she put me off, the more desperate I felt for her, the more I knew I loved her.

Wednesday morning I awoke to pouring rain. It flooded all through the morning. The paddock and the ring were a sloshy, brown mess. What wasn't brown was gray and dreary. The hunt club was a miserable place when it rained. All of the lessons I had booked for the morning cancelled and the afternoon hunt was cancelled too. That disappointed me.

Thomson wasn't a tiny town, but it was the kind of town that was rooted in tradition. One of these traditions was beginning to fade as was many of the businesses were doing away with the half work day on Wednesdays. This was yet to touch the members of the hunt. They were so accustomed to coming to the hunt on Wednesday afternoons that many of them didn't know what else to do with themselves so they showed up at the barn anyway. Mr. Watson was one of those that showed up that afternoon.

"Edward," he called my name as I passed by Blueberry's stall.

"Yes, sir?" I stepped back to the stall door. I found Mr. Watson grooming Blueberry himself.

Mr. Watson had visibly aged in this last year. His hair was thinner and the gray was more visible. I remembered what Lily had told me. Mrs. Watson, Lucy's mother, was pregnant. He was forty-four as well and about to be a father again. I just couldn't imagine my parents having a baby at their age.

"Has Lucy been around to sign up for lessons yet?" He continued to brush Blueberry's mane as we spoke.

"No, sir."

"Ahh," he grunted.

"She's busy at the kennel. I'm sure she'd got more important things to do." I reached for the tack bucket and offered to help him.

"No, I don't mind doing this myself. I rather enjoy it."

"Alright. Well, yell if you need anything."

I started to walk off when Mr. Watson called to me again. "Edward."

"Yes, sir," again I stepped back to the gate.

"What are you doing for dinner?" He glanced up from his task.

I hesitated and that was enough of an indication for him that I had no plans so he invited me, more like insisted, that I come to dinner at their house.

"That settles it. Dinner's at 6:30 p.m., but you can get there any time before that."

"I really don't want to impose." The fact of the matter was that I didn't want to endure an awkward evening across the table from Lucy and I didn't want her to endure it either. I'd been there so much for dinner last year that turning him down now would be awkward as well.

Mr. Watson took his eyes off of Blueberry again. "You're not imposing. The girls have taken over cooking duties and it's Lucy's night. She's a way better cook than Lily, but she seems to think she's preparing for an army."

I couldn't contain the urge to laugh at the thought of Lucy cooking.

"Of course I would deny it if you ever told, but I'd rather have the leftovers from Lucy's meal than most anything Lily cooked fresh." He turned up his nose and made a gagging gesture.

"What happened to Molly and why isn't she helping you all out with the cooking since Mrs. Watson's..."

"That's another sore subject altogether."

Mr. Watson wiped his brow and Blueberry rolled her lips and huffed. Mr. Watson couldn't seem to talk and brush Blueberry down at the same time and Blueberry didn't seem to like that he'd stopped.

Mr. Watson continued, "Molly's no longer with us. Mary, Lucy's mother..." I knew who he was talking about, but he clarified anyway. "She thought it was high time Lily was done having a paid companion. She felt that as long as Molly was around Lily wouldn't live up to her potential. Ultimately, Molly and Mary butted heads and someone had to go. Women," he shrugged.

I wanted to commiserate, but how could I commiserate with him about his wife and daughters. I just stood there listening while he went on.

"I walked in the house one day and thought I was about to witness a good ol' fashioned cat fight. Mary told Molly to her face that there was a new bitch in town. I could hardly believe it. Molly gathered her purse and hasn't been back. Lily was broken hearted at first, but Mary trotted her off to the doctor and secured a clean bill of health for her. Mary then told Lily that she was old enough to do better than what she was doing and there was no reason for her to stay laid up on her father forever. For a moment I thought Lily was going to be the next one grabbing her purse and running for the hills."

My concern was, "Where was Lucy in all of this?"

"School, hiding in her room, working at the kennel or helping the ladies of the hunt redecorate your apartment. She practically did all of the work on the apartment herself. She spent so much time there I got a little worried she was planning on moving in."

I took Lucy's involvement in the redecorating as a sign that she still cared for me. Why else would she have taken such an interest?

Mr. Watson went on to tell me that after Lily's clean bill of health Mary inquired as to the possibility of Lily gaining some weight and starting to lead the normal life of a twenty year old girl. "Thanks to Mary's efforts, the oncologist referred Lily to a nutritionist, who organized a diet for Lily to put on weight and start gaining muscle mass. She then took Lily to a personal trainer that was recommended by the nutritionist and for six months it was Lily's full time job to get herself in shape."

Mr. Watson gave up on finishing with Blueberry and started returning all of the tack to the bucket while he told me about Lily. "At first Lily was resistant and resentful that Molly was gone. Mary didn't give up or back down. She told Lily that everyone was expected to do something with their lives and she was no exception. I felt caught in the middle, but Mary had been after me for years to, in her words, 'Make Lily get off her ass.' Turns out Lily, just needed a little motivation. Mary asked her, 'Do you want to have a family of your own one day? If the answer is yes, then you better start working for it. Nothing in life's free.' Before I knew it, Lily was going to the gym, eating like a grown man and she was not staggering everywhere anymore."

I could sense a little bit pride in his voice. "You've got to be proud of Mary and Lily."

"Oh, of course. Mary pushed her and Lily rose to the occasion." Mr. Watson sat the tack bucket down and stood there for a moment, gathering more thoughts. "I must say, I'm disappointed in myself that I let Lily waste so much of her life. If I had only believed in her the way Mary has and pushed like Mary pushed the girls, there's no telling what Lily could have made of herself. I feel like I did Lily a disservice."

I knew their family history from last year and how Lily's mother died when Lily was very little. I knew how he was left to raise a small, sickly child all by himself. "I don't think you should beat yourself up. I think you did the best you could."

I couldn't imagine my father not losing his mind and leaving us if he was in that situation. I also couldn't imagine having these types of conversations with my father, conversations where he showed vulnerability or admitted where he felt he went wrong with us or in life. I felt these sorts of admission showed just what a good father Mr. Watson was. I envied both Lily and Lucy for having him for a father. I knew from the time I met him there's nothing he wouldn't do for his children and he always had what he thought were their best interests in mind.

He made one more confession, "You know, I would have taken care of Lily for her entire life, but I see now that. I failed at teaching her to take care of herself. Thank Heavens for Mary and how she has rectified my shortcomings."

Before I knew what I said, I told Mr. Watson how I envied his daughters.

"Thank you and, I don't know why, but as far as I'm concerned when you are in town, I see you as one of mine too."

I felt my cheeks flush. "Thank you, sir. It really means a lot to hear you say that." There was no way to decline the invitation to dinner at the Watson's after that exchange.

The rain slacked off around 5:00 p.m., just in time for me to get dressed for dinner and head over. Mr. Watson mentioned to Lucy that a guest was coming for dinner, but he didn't mention to her that the guest was me. He also didn't tell me that when Lucy made dinner she plated everyone's food up and set it out like a server at a restaurant.

I found myself at the dinner table with silverware in place, napkin and a glass of sweet tea set out the same for me as it was for everyone else at the table. The only thing missing was the plate and the dishes of food.

Our seating arrangement was the same as last year. Mr. Watson was at the head of the table and Lily sat to his left. Mrs. Mary was allowed a reprieve from bedrest to join in meals so she was seated to Mr. Watson's right. I was seated next to Lily again and there was a place setting across from me and next to Mrs. Mary that was for Lucy.

"Edward, it's so good to see you," Mrs. Mary said as she took her seat. She was huge and I had to put forth the effort not to stare.

"It's good to see you too and thank you so much for having me." I was absolutely parched and reached for my tea.

Lily chimed in, "I tried to get him to come sooner, but he didn't want to impose. Can you imagine him imposing?" Lily winked at me and smiled.

"You're welcome here anytime," Mr. Watson added.

In the midst of our small talk Lucy entered the room wearing a grease splattered apron and carrying two plates of food. She stopped in her tracks and almost dropped the plates. This is when I realized they had not shared with her that I was the guest for dinner. She recovered, but again gritted her teeth and shot me the "eat shit and die" look.

"Look who's come to dinner," Mr. Watson said proudly.

"I see," snapped Lucy as she slung the first plate in front of her mother and the second in front of Lily. She glared at me, "Ladies first."

Perhaps she was still trying to make the point to me about manners, like the other night when she told me, "Girls don't call boys."

Lucy stormed back in the kitchen and returned with two more plates. The first of those she put in front of her vacant seat and the second she sat in front of her father. She returned to the kitchen and a few minutes passed before she came back with another plate.

Lucy slid the last plate in front of me and in a voice daring me to eat it she said, "Enjoy!"

Who knew the word "enjoy" was polite for "you asshole"? Apparently it was. It was a loaded down plate of fried shrimp, green beans, scalloped potatoes and cocktail sauce, but thanks to the tone of the word and due to the length of time she stayed in the kitchen before bringing out my dinner, I was scared to eat it.

All through dinner there was polite conversation about how Lily had taken over as Mr. Watson's secretary, whether Mrs. Mary was having a boy or another girl and how Lucy had outdone herself with dinner tonight. Lucy sat defiantly chewing and I pushed the pieces of shrimp around on my plate. I was so hungry and the shrimp were fried golden brown and they smelled so good. I wanted to eat it, but I kept thinking about Whitney Knox going head over heels into the ditch last summer.

Lily noticed me playing with my food. "Edward, is there something wrong?"

"Oh, nothing, I had a late lunch." I lied.

The conversation continued and Lucy refused to participate or look at me. I took that as a challenge. I became determined to make her speak to me and look at me. After all else failed, I ran my foot gently up her leg. I received a swift kick, a blow to my shin, which I had not expected. Lucy had the kick of a mule and I flinched, knocked my knee into the table. The table took a jolting and everyone screamed as Mrs. Mary's tea flew over and spilled in her lap.

Mr. Watson jumped into action helping Mary with the spill. Lily ran to the kitchen for more paper towels. The glass of tea had just been topped off and Mrs. Mary was ringing wet. She insisted on going up stairs to change. Mr. Watson guided his very pregnant wife out of the room.

Both Lucy and I had sprang to aid in the cleanup and now we were the only ones left in the room. The volume of tea that was in Mrs. Mary's lap was equal to that still on the table. All of us had thrown our napkins into the liquid, but they were of little help. Lucy and I busied ourselves picking up ice cubes, both of us reaching from across the table.

Lucy began berating me. "What are you doing here?"

"Your father invited me."

"Jesus, why can't he mind his own business?" That was a long standing complaint that Lucy had about Mr. Watson.

"Because you are his business."

"Ugh!" She grunted and rolled her eyes at me.

Lucy and I both reach for the same piece of ice at the same time. My hand landed on top of hers. She tried to snatch hers back, but I didn't let her.

"Ask me why I didn't call," I dared her.

I felt alive just touching her. I didn't want to tell her about Anne, but I wanted her back so badly I would have told her anything. Anything, but she had to ask.

"No. I don't care why you didn't call!" Still, she didn't move her hand.

"You know how I felt about you. I know you felt something for me." I studied her eyes. "Don't you want to know what happened?"

Lucy eased her hand back, shaking her head like she was trying to rid herself of a nasty thought. "It's not important anymore." Her tone wasn't defiant like it had been in the parking lot of the hunt club the night we last fought. Tonight her tone was defeated and sad. I had broken her heart and I hated myself for it.

Chapter 9

The days and nights were long. I went to work and came back to the apartment. My life now existed in about a hundred yard radius. I didn't even go to town to get dinner. Since I had arrived back in Thomson each lady that took a lesson gave me some baked good or another. The chicken casserole that Mrs. Harper brought me the first night lasted a week and one of the other ladies brought me another. I wasn't worried about being fed.

Saturday arrived. It was my first day off in two weeks. When I wasn't giving lessons, I was cleaning tack and scrubbing down the stalls and the barn as a whole.

The ladies had spared no expense in redecorating the apartment, except on the curtains. These things were paper thin and the one day I didn't have to get up early I was forced up by the rising sun.

I was not to be cheated out of my sleep. I got up and pulled out the winter blankets from the shelf in the closet and sat them on the bed while I went to fish out the thumbtacks I remembered seeing in one of the kitchen drawers. I came back with tacks in hand and covered the windows with someone's handmade quilt. I cut the window unit down and dove back into the bed. I was just about asleep again when the phone rang.

"Hello?" Translation, "You just woke me up!"

"Hey!" It was Lily and she was entirely too chipper. "What are you doing tonight?"

"I don't know. Nothing, I guess." I pulled the covers over my head while I waited for whatever it was she was about to require of me.

"Good. That settles it. You're coming with me to Lucy's party."

"Jesus Christ," I mumbled.

It had been three days since I'd seen Lucy. I saw her Mustang at the kennel every day, but I made a point to avoid going down there. I believe she was making the same point about coming up to the barn. We'd done a fine job of avoiding one another, but it wasn't helping me.

"What?" It was good Lily didn't understand my initial answer.

"No. I don't think I should." This time I voiced my reply in a more sensible tone. The thought of going to Lucy's birthday party and seeing Wilson Knox all over her actually made loneliness more appealing.

"I won't take no for an answer. It's not a date, but I'll pick you up at 7:00 p.m."

"You'll pick me up?" Last summer she had a driver and still didn't have her own driver's license or anything. In fact, last summer she was so frail I don't think she could have physically managed the task of pressing the gas pedal.

"Yes. I can't wait for you to see my new car!"

"No, Lily, I really shouldn't. I don't think Lucy would want me there."

"Oh, please! You're all she talks about. Mind you, she's really steamed with you, but still, she'll get over it."

I hoped Lucy would get over it, but I wasn't so sure.

"Fine. 7:00. I'll be ready, but don't honk the horn and think I'll run out." I made the joke and it went right over Lily's head. I was also amused that Lily seemed perfectly fine with picking up boys, but Lucy couldn't bring herself to call one.

"Okay. It's just up at the Halfway House..."

I don't know what Lily said after that. At some point we said goodbye to one another, but the rest of the conversation was one sided, hers, and it amounted to background noise for my thoughts. The Halfway House, I remembered it well. Thinking of the party there last year is what got me through this past winter.

I was somewhere between catnapping and dreaming of kissing Lucy at the Halfway House, when the phone rang for the second time that morning. I caught it on the second ring. It was Mrs. Harper and she wanted to know if I would like to earn a little extra money. Of course I would.

By 8:30 a.m. I was at the Harper's getting a crash course in bush hogging. Mr. Harper normally did this himself, but with his back out the tractor seat was not his friend.

"Sorry about Mr. Harper. How did he hurt his back?" I asked Mrs. Harper as she checked the fluids in the tractor engine.

Mrs. Harper stopped momentarily and began the story. She blushed as she recounted his accident. "He was getting out of the garden tub and slipped."

"Oh, that's terrible."

"That's not even the worst of it. He grabbed the shower curtain for something to save him, but his weight was too much for that. The rings popped from the rod and when it all gave way. It twisted him around and he fell head first between the wall and the toilet."

"Now you know he's a Clydesdale of a man," Mrs. Harper held her hands fairly wide apart demonstrating how big of a fella Mr. Harper was. She went on, "And he managed to wedge himself into a spot about this big." She brought her hands back together with the span of about a foot between them.

"Oh," I didn't know what else to say. I was starting to form a mental picture.

"I was on the far end of the house and heard the commotion and went running to see if half of the house had caved in. You know how I found him?"

She didn't give me time to answer. "Upside down, naked as a jay bird with his legs and feet kicking in the air. He was good 'n stuck."

It was all I could do not to double over laughing. Mrs. Harper painted quite an image. I kept it together enough to ask, "How did you get him free?"

"Well, it wasn't easy, I'll tell you that. His pride being what it is, he wouldn't let me call anyone to come help us. He barely agreed to let me call you to help with the field today. I struggled pulling on him and trying to turn him. I tugged on him for a half hour before I gave up and got the butter."

"The butter?"

"I greased him like a pig, used my entire container of Country Crock before he slipped loose."

I knew what Mr. Harper looked like and the thought of her lathering him up with butter was too much. My insides were about to explode. I had to laugh.

"I know!" She laughed with me. "I can't hardly look at him without picturing his ass in the air and his legs kicking and I haven't been able to eat butter since."

Before Mrs. Harper turned me loose on the tractor, she struck up one more conversation. "Edward, do you have a girlfriend back home?"

"No, ma'am."

"I've been thinking. You know who would be perfect for you?" She let the engine cover down and took off her work gloves.

I feared she was going to tell me she had some granddaughter that I had yet to meet. I stood silent waiting as I knew it was a rhetorical question.

While using one of her gloves to wipe her brow, Mrs. Harper told me who she had in mind. "I think you should ask out Lucy Meeks. I think she's just the prettiest and sweetest thing around."

"I don't know. I think I'm a bit old for her."

Mrs. Harper gave me a knowing look, "I've seen the way you look at her."

I crossed my arms and stood my ground. "Really and how's that?"

"Same as all the other men and boys around when she walks by." She gave me a pat on the arm. "You can't fool me. Plus, you know how much older I am than Bud? About five years. Age hasn't got a thing to do with it. Anyway, let's see if we can fire up this tractor and get you daydreaming about Miss Meeks."

I felt the need to point out, "I think she's got a boyfriend."

"Like you couldn't steal any girl away from scrawny little Wilson Knox. He's barely out of short britches."

"You know you are bad."

"I wear it with pride." Mrs. Harper laughed. "Now, you take my advice and ask that girl out."

Randomly throughout the day while riding the bush-hogger, the image of Mr. Harper wedged upside down would pop in my head and I would burst out laughing all over again. Just as randomly, I revisited the conversation about Lucy. Little did Mrs. Harper know, Lucy and I had a bit of a history and it wasn't as simple as just asking her out on a date. I wish it was that simple, but it wasn't.

When I was finished Mrs. Harper offered me a hundred dollar bill and a pan of lasagna. I refused her money, but I gladly accepted the lasagna. As good as the Harpers had been to me, I didn't feel right about taking the money. Mrs. Harper was one of the best cooks of all of the ladies in the hunt. I wasn't about to turn down a meal from her kitchen.

That evening Lily showed up at the exact moment she said she would. I had just finished pulling on one of my Thomas Jackson College t-shirts when the knocking at the door began. Lily came to the door and knocked just the way I had insisted when I teased her earlier that morning. Each time I laid eyes on her it was hard to reconcile the girl before me with the girl from last summer. She had not just gained weight, but she'd put on some muscle tone. There was more of a resemblance between her and Lucy now than ever before. Anyone who didn't recognize that they were blood related sisters was a fool.

Although I grabbed my keys and locked the door behind us, I still didn't feel right about going. I also felt a little underdressed considering Lily was wearing a sparkling party dress and I was wearing jeans and a T-shirt. I was no frills and she was all frills. Based on our contrasting attire, I felt the need to confirm again, "Are you sure I won't be crashing the party?"

"No. You're with me. It will be fine." Lily grabbed me by the hand and pulled me down the steps.

Lily's car was a far cry from the antique Mustang Lucy drove. Sitting in the driveway next to my Bronco was Lily's brand new Volkswagen Cabriolet. White and convertible, it reminded me of the Barbie Car Anne had as a child. She played with that thing even after the wheels fell off.

Seemed like something that represented Anne's memory was everywhere I turned here at the Wrightsboro Hunt. Lily's car was not the only thing that night that brought her memory to the forefront of my mind. Anne's first job had been here at the hunt and folks still remembered her and asked me about her from time to time. In fact, Anne and Lily had been good friends and it was only when I got in the car that I thought about the fact that they had lost touch and Lily didn't know what happened.

I tried to take my mind of off Anne and said the first thing that came to mind. "I guess Wilson Knox will be here tonight."

"He likes to be called 'Will' now," Lily answered as she made the turn from the driveway onto the road. "And, yes, he's supposed to be there."

"Figures," I said under my breath.

I could have gone the rest of the half mile trip in silence, but Lily would have none of that. "I think my dad's got Lucy a new horse for her birthday."

"What's wrong with Blueberry?" I looked at her. Lucy loved that horse.

"Nothing," Lily was almost offended by my question. "Other than she's my horse."

"Oh, right." I'd forgotten about that detail.

"I mentioned she might like her own horse. Daddy thought it was a nice idea."

"You know she loves that horse."

"She'll love her new horse, too."

I let out an exasperated sigh and didn't say anything else the rest of the way there. Lily went on and on about the new horse, but it made me sad for Blueberry and Lucy. I could never tell what Lily's intentions were toward Lucy. Was she jealous? Lily had led a very sheltered, catered to life and then last year her whole world was upended. It had to be hard finding out that her father had fathered another child, even if the child was one of your dear friends. It must have been hard on her that suddenly she wasn't the woman of the house any more. To look at her one would think she'd adjusted well, but these little things she slid into conversations made me think otherwise. The way she told me about Wilson Knox to begin with and reminding me that Blueberry was hers, those were two examples that made me wonder what was really going on with her. It made me wonder why she'd insisted I come to this party for Lucy. She lived in the house with Lucy. She had to know that Lucy basically hated me right now.

We pulled up the driveway of the Halfway House with me giving Lily a once over. What was she thinking? What was she up to?

"Well, we're here. Time to make our grand entrance." Lily shut of the car and got out.

"Excuse me?" I stood up and looked over the hood of the car.

"We're fashionably late. You know..."

"That's the thing, I think I do know." I had two sisters and I was starting to get the idea. Anne and B were one another's biggest rivals. "You go on in. I don't feel right about this. I'm just going to walk back home. Plus, I didn't get her a gift."

"You know, you're never going to get her back as long as you're hiding out in the barn." Maybe I'd gotten the wrong idea about Lily's intentions. If she still wanted me for herself, or to rub it in with Lucy that I was her date, surely she wouldn't have advised me on what to do to get Lucy back.

Lily was right. I would never get Lucy back if I kept avoiding her. She was also right about us making an entrance. We did that alright. All eyes in the living room were on us. Mostly the attention was due to Lily's transformation.

I scoped out the pathway from the foyer to the living room, taking in my surroundings. From what I could tell, there were as many adult members of the hunt and friends of Mr. Watson there, as there were teenage friends of Lucy's at the party this year. I wasn't necessarily looking for Lucy, but there she was. I noticed her as soon as we stepped in the living room.

I didn't feel underdressed anymore. Lucy was wearing a snug tank top and jeans. The jeans were the contradiction of new and old at the same time. The color indicated they were new, but the purposefully placed rips tried to give the illusion that they were well worn. This was the new style. From head to toe I looked her over. The strappy silver heels were a classy touch to an otherwise casual look. She wasn't just beautiful tonight, Lucy was sexy.

Lucy was standing in the doorway between the living room and the kitchen chatting with her best friend Maggie McCorkle and Wilson. I'd met Maggie a couple of times last year. Both Maggie and Wilson were laughing over whatever Lucy said, but Wilson's laugh was loud and obnoxious. The more I took note of him, the more obnoxious everything about him seemed to me.

It wasn't the spectacle made by Wilson that made me notice them. It was as if the Gates of Heaven opened when I turned in her direction. There was no double take needed. Lucy virtually glowed. The light from the room caught the gloss on her lips and they sparkled. I would have died a thousand deaths to kiss those lips and the wonder of whether I would ever be able to do that again, kiss them, made the pit of my stomach ache.

Lucy was no longer laughing with them. She'd spotted me. As everyone gushed over Lily, like it was her coming out party, the birthday girl cut her eyes at me. With Wilson Knox hanging over her shoulders like a coat, she was looking at me and I was looking at her.

With a pissed look on her face Lucy slipped the grasp of Will or Wilson or whatever he was calling himself and started toward me from the far side of the living room. I gathered she was on her way to throw me out or have yet another showdown.

Lucy had commented a time or two that she envied Maggie's red hair and fair skin, but Maggie had nothing on Lucy in the way of looks. Maggie was a pretty girl, but Lucy was the fire. Even mad, she was breathtakingly gorgeous.

Last year Lucy described her mother as being the homecoming queen when she was in her teens and that Mr. Watson described her as the best looking girl in the county. Well, the apple certainly didn't fall far from the tree.

Her hair was chestnut brown with streaks of copper and she had it pinned up in a bun on the back of her head. Locks fell loose around her face. She never wore much more than lip gloss or spent more than five minutes on her looks whereas girls like my sister B would have spent hours trying to accomplish her look. I couldn't imagine there was a boy or a man around that would turn her down.

The tank top, the low slung jeans, she wasn't rake thin and she wasn't curvy either. I tried not to stare, but how anyone could keep from looking at her was beyond me.

The best part of Lucy wasn't her hair or that she was the perfect size or shape. The best part of Lucy was that she had no idea how attractive she really was and each time someone told her it was a surprise to her. She was the picture of grace and humility, except for right that minute and she was coming for me.

I stood firm as Lucy approached and took in the sight of her. I day dreamed of nuzzling into her neck and falling asleep to the smell of her hair. She was almost to me when a hand was laid gently on my forearm. The touch came in the on the opposite side from my gaze at Lucy. I thought it was Lily, but then the words came.

Chapter 10

"Edward, I was so sorry to hear about your sister Anne."

My heart sank. Of course that distracted me from whatever onslaught was about to come from Lucy. I dropped the eye contact with her and turned to see from whom the condolences were coming. As far as I knew, the news of Anne had not reached Thomson. I was wrong in that assumption.

I found Sylvia Pate, the wife of the current master of the Wrightsboro Hunt, shaking her head. She still had the wrapped present she'd brought for Lucy in one hand as the other remained on my arm. She gave a couple of pats as she spoke.

"I can't even imagine the loss of a child." Mrs. Pate was clearly picturing herself in my parents' predicament. "Your parents must be devastated. You must be devastated. Did they ever find the person..."

She wasn't really finished with the question, but I knew it all to well as most everyone asked the same thing. "No ma'am, they haven't."

"Oh, I am so sorry. If there's anything I can do."

"Thank you so much and please just pray they catch him," I told her. "Closure would mean a lot to my parents. It won't bring her back, but my mother seems to think knowing what exactly happened to her and who did it would bring some peace."

"Of course I'll definitely keep y'all in my prayers."

Last year I was always acutely in tune to Lucy's proximity to me. I didn't even have to see her back then for my heart to race. Last year I could have felt her near, but not this time. I was completely surprised when Mrs. Pate spoke to her and I realized she had been standing there for the entire conversation.

"Lucy, it's so good to see you." Mrs. Pate's voice lifted. "Happy birthday, sweetie." She handed Lucy the present.

Lucy had the wherewithal to take the big box Mrs. Pate shoved into her, but she didn't take her eyes off of me. Her words caught in her throat, she barely opened her mouth and a confused "Thank you" fell out.

"Ah, I see Master Pate about to get in the punch. I know that's not sugar free. Let me go stop him before helps himself to a diabetic coma." Mrs. Pate left and it was just me and Lucy and she couldn't seem to get her jaw off of the floor.

Lucy sat the package down on the table next to the couch that was where Lily had taken a seat and was entertaining everyone with stories of how she'd beaten cancer. And what Lucy's mother had put her through to improve her physically over the last year. Suddenly it was as if Lucy and I were the only people in the room. All of the other party guests faded away.

"I had no idea." Lucy's eyes were brimming with tears. "Why didn't you tell me?"

I rubbed my face, doing that thing I did when I was frustrated or in a difficult spot. This was definitely a difficult spot.

"I don't want to talk about it now. I don't want to ruin your party."

Lucy wouldn't take her eyes off of me. She studied me for answers. All I would say is, "Now's not the time."

Lucy looked around. The guest were mingling and the music was playing and the whole house was alive. It was a dream party for any girl in this area, but the look on Lucy's face was that of desperation to escape it. She shook her head and looked back at me. "Wait five minutes and then meet me. You know the place."

I did indeed know the place.

I went out the front door and made the same trip around the side of the Halfway House to the back. The same route I made last year. I arrived first and it took Lucy longer to come down through the basement. Five minutes passed and I kept waiting. Another five passed and I stood there under the overhang.

Last year it was pouring buckets, but tonight there wasn't a cloud in the sky and it was beautiful. I watched the sky as I waited for Lucy to come down. The one thing about the land near the Wrightsboro Hunt Club is that it had the best view of the night's sky I'd ever seen. The club's property was far enough from town that there was none of what folks referred to back home as "light pollution."

The minutes ticked by and, to keep from worrying that she wasn't coming and that this was her trick to get me out of her party, I began counting the stars. I was on number one hundred and thirteen when I heard the creaking of the old back door being opened. It was Lucy. I reached out to her, but she refused my hand.

She kept her words to a whisper and, again, I was reminded of last year. On one hand it seemed like a lifetime ago, but on the other, it seemed like only yesterday.

"What happened to your sister?"

Everyone back home knew what happened and I'd never had to explain to anyone before. I'd never had to say the words out loud before. If I didn't spit them out now, I wouldn't be able to say them at all. "She was kidnapped and murdered and God only knows what else in between."

Lucy gasped and covered her mouth with both hands. I gave her a moment to process what I said before I added anything.

"They never found who took her."

"Your younger sister?" She sought to confirm.

"Yes." I stiffened and tried to put on a brave face for Lucy.

"Oh my God, Edward!" Lucy just shook her head. "I'm so sorry."

"No, I'm sorry, Lucy." I reached out and ran my hand across her cheek and tucked a strand of hair behind her ear. It was an intimate touch and she didn't recoil. "I should have told you, but I blamed myself for what happened to Anne and..."

"When did this happen?"

That was the million dollar question that I really didn't want to answer. Even though there'd been a time when I blamed Lucy for distracting me that night, I never wanted her to know it. I answered with the historical name of the day, hoping Lucy wouldn't connect the date as the last time we spoke. "Pearl Harbor Day."

My attempt was in vain.   Lucy was quick. "December 7?"

"Yes."

I could see the wheels turning in her head. "She went missing on the night we last spoke?"

I nodded. There was a stretch of silence. I don't think Lucy knew what to make of this so I decided it was best just to shut the conversation down. "Don't you need to get back to your party?"

Lucy ran her hands through her hair, exasperated. "Forget the party! Tell me exactly what happened."

I slumped against the wall behind me. "We were   at   the   concert   and   I   left..." "No! No! No!" Lucy started to cry. She was a very bright girl and I didn't have to finish the statement before she jumped to the conclusion. "You left her to call me?"

"Yes and when I came back, I couldn't find her."

"No, Edward, I am so sorry. I don't know what else to say."

I pulled Lucy into my chest. "Lucy, it's my fault. I should have never left her. I should have told you sooner. I'll tell you all of the details I know, but don't make me ruin your night."

Lucy gripped on to the back of my shirt at my shoulder blades by the handful and held tight. I stroked her head as I cradled her in my arms.

Lucy raised her head and, with the pad of my thumb, I wiped the tear from under her right eye. "Let's get you dried up so you can get back to your

party. Wilson's probably wondering where you are."
I tried to say and do the right thing in the moment.

She gave me a slight smile and she stepped back from me. She dabbed off her face. "I'm so sorry about Anne. I'm sorry I've been cruel to you lately."

"There's nothing for you to be sorry about. It's me that owes you the biggest apology and I am so, so sorry, Lucy. I've been such a coward when it came to you and you don't deserve that."

I thought she was about to head back inside, but Lucy reached for my hand. Just to feel her touch made my heart stop.

"You were right, I should have called you." She squeezed my hand as she spoke.

More than anything I wanted to ask Lucy if there was a chance for us. I wanted to know if I had a chance. Clearly there was something with her and Wilson Knox or she wouldn't have let him cling to her the way he did. I never pictured her as liking that sort of attention, but how would I know? All last summer we had to sneak around so there was never any inclination that she might like public displays of affection.

I held my tongue and let her go back to the party. I watched her until she disappeared thought the door before I turned to leave.

"Edward," Lucy stuck her head back out. "You aren't leaving are you?"

"Yeah, but not before I go back in and say goodbye to Lily."

"I'd like it if you'd stay, but I understand if you're not in the mood to be at a party tonight."

"I don't know."

"Well, at least come in and have one dance with the birthday girl. She's always wondered what it would be like to dance with you." Lucy smiled as she referred to herself in the third person.

I hung my head. "I thought the birthday girl hated me." I wouldn't have blamed her if she did.

"No. She could never hate you." Lucy gave an affirming nod. "And, Edward, you can come back in this way. You don't have to walk all the way around. There's no need to sneak around this year."

"Are you sure?"

Lucy held out her hand to me. Glancing from my hand to her as I took it, I definitely felt encouragement coming from her. There was hope. The frost that was between us melted and I could feel the old us in my grasp.

She gave me one more smile before leading me back inside. That smile would stay locked in my mind forever. The way the moonlight lit her face was like an old black and white photo. It took all I could not to pull her back to me and kiss her. It would be the kind of kiss that made up for lost time. I resisted, but had to adjust myself while going up the stairs or else all of her party guest would have known that my struggle to resist was real and it was raging.

Lucy stopped on the top step and turned around to me. We were eye to eye and it was a cramped space. Being that close to her did nothing to help the situation I was having containing my emotions. She put her hands on my shoulders and for a second, I thought she was going to initiate something. Instead, she said, "Just don't leave before I have my dance." Then, she opened the door and went back to her friends.

The furniture that usually sat in the living room, the couch and arm chairs, were moved to the edge of the room to make way for the dance floor. I found Lily sitting in one of the chairs listening to Mr. Watson go on about the breeding of Lucy's new horse. I took a seat on the arm of her chair. Turned out Blueberry was going to be a mother and the foal was to be Lucy's. I'm not sure why Lily didn't just tell me that to begin with, but I didn't say anything.

As I sat there listening to the stories Mr. Watson told about horse breeding, I found out that Blueberry was actually the product of his childhood horse and one he had given his first wife as a wedding present. I also noticed that the music playing was all from the eighties. I commented on the music to Lily.

Lily advised, "Oh, yeah, Lucy's favorite music is from the eighties. She's a big Duran Duran and Genesis fan. Oh, and Pearl Jam. Jesus, I hear that coming through the walls every night."

I chuckled. "Is she now?"

"I can't tell you how my ears bleed at night listening to those two bands and power ballads over and over again." Lily pulled me down to her level so no one else would hear. "I swear, if you ever break her heart again, I'll do that 'Say Anything' scene with the boom box outside of your window and you will have to endure it too. Don't test me."

"I promise, I won't break her heart again."

"Good."

I excused myself and went to the DJ who was stationed in the opposite corner. I figured if Lucy was a fan of the group Genesis, then she was probably a fan of Phil Collins' solo music.

My mother's favorite movie was White Nights. "The finest ballet movie ever made," she'd tell me as she watched it over and over again. It was the first VHS tape we owned. The theme song to the movie was "Separate Lives" by Phil Collins and that's what I asked the DJ if he had as I slid him a ten dollar bill from my wallet.

He could hardly hear me above the speakers that were in front of his table and between us. He nodded in response.

"Would you please play that next?"

Again, he nodded as reached for the money.

I started back to my seat on the arm of Lily's chair unsure if he had the song or if he'd just taken my money.

"Hey, man, I can't play it next. The birthday girl requested a special one next," the DJ yelled at me and I heard him despite the thumping speaker between us.

A couple of licks of the guitar and before that calling type sound Eddie Vedar let out at the beginning of the song, I knew what Lucy had requested, "Black" by Pearl Jam. I hardly had to turn my head and there she was.

"Dance with me."

I hung my head and shook off a laugh. "Of course."

It was mostly Lucy's friends that were dancing and the adults were milling around between the kitchen and dining room or sitting in the corner of the living room. Lucy led me out among her friends. Maggie and her date were among them, but Wilson Knox was nowhere to be found.

Lucy and I started off a safe distance apart. She slid her hands up my arms cautiously until they came to rest on my shoulders. We swayed back and forth in little circles, but as the song played on Lucy's hands inched up and her arms draped around my neck. She was wearing heels, but she was still so tiny in my arms.

The more the music went on the closer we got, our bodies pressed against one another. We were no longer a safe distance apart and certainly not an appropriate distance apart with her father potentially watching our every move. It was the thought of him watching that kept my hands on the small of her back. I was failing at that, but I didn't let them go any farther than the waistband of her jeans.

"I take a walk outside..." I'm no singer, but I started to sing along with Pearl Jam. I knew all the words to the song. I'd played it a million times since Lucy first told me that it was playing the first time she saw me. Some people think guys aren't sentimental, and they are right about some guys, but I'm not one of those guys especially when it came to the people I cared about.

We swayed together like a tree bending gently with the wind. Her eyes were closed and she held me tightly just going with the flow of the music.

Before I let go of Lucy at the end of the song I whispered to her, "I don't want you to be the sun in somebody else's sky. You're the sun in my sky. You always have been."

Lucy smiled and slinked away without saying anything. I didn't know what to think. She disappeared into the crowd by the foyer.

The song I requested started and after Lucy just left me standing there I couldn't bear the thought of hearing it. I wasn't sure where she went, maybe to find Wilson, but I wasn't sticking around to find out.

I said my goodbyes to Lily, interrupting her from holding court with Mr. Watson and his friends. Lily offered to drive me, but I insisted she stay at the party.

"Don't let my weird mood ruin your night," I told her.

"Are you sure?" Lily was so sweet and clearly no longer interested in me, which was a relief. That would have been the cherry on top of this already awkward night.

"I'm sure. I'm just going to walk back. The night air will do me good."

"Alright. I feel bad about not taking you home."

"Don't. I'm a big boy. I'll get over this, whatever it is."

"Hey," Lily reached out and patted my hand. "Hang in there and trust me. She'll come around."

Clearly Lily knew something I didn't. All I knew was that Lucy seemed to be on some sort of emotional teeter totter with me.

My overly dramatic choice in songs had run everyone off of the make shift dance floor. As I stepped out onto the small porch of the Halfway House I saw where they had gone.

A small group had gathered near Lucy's car, the first one in the row of cars parked outside of the house.

"We're done!" a male voice screamed.

118

"Fine!" I couldn't see her, but a voice distinctly Lucy's shouted back.

"How could you do me like that? Seriously, two timing me with the stable boy?" I hadn't recognized the voice at first, but I did now. It was Wilson and he was fuming mad with Lucy.

He charged at her and I started down the stairs. If he laid a hand on her I'd beat his scrawny ass. I was stopped at the bottom step by Maggie.

Maggie grabbed my arm. "Just let it play out. She'll be okay. He won't touch her."

"I'm sorry. It's just..." Lucy started to explain and I continued to watch.

Wilson cut her off, "Save it! I don't care!" He gave her a dismissive wave of his hand. "He can have you!"

It appeared I'd won and Wilson Knox was history, but there was something off about that entire exchange. Whatever it was, I had a feeling this wasn't the time to claim my prize.

"Please tell Lucy I said 'Happy Birthday' and that I had to go home," I asked Maggie.

"Sure. It was good to see you, Edward, and for what it's worth, I'm sorry about your sister." Maggie gave me a hug and I got on my way without further notice.

Word seemed to be getting around about Anne.

Chapter 11

I rubbed my eyes to see the glowing red numbers on the alarm clock. "11:08," I exhaled. I'd been asleep for an hour.

I perked up. There it was again. The banging. "What was that?" I whispered to myself.

The bed in my room was way more comfortable than the one from last year. I had been in a deep sleep and it was good. It took me a minute to come to and realize what was going on. The only light in the room was from the clock.

I felt around for my shirt, but couldn't find it. I gave up when the hammering on the door started again. I got out of bed and started toward the origin of the sound in nothing but my boxers.

In all the time I'd stayed in the apartment no one had ever come up there during the night before. The way whomever was there was wailing on the door made me think there might be an emergency or something.

I cut the lamp on as I passed through the living room. I got all the way to the door before I heard her, "Edward, it's Lucy. Let me in."

"Lucy?" I questioned through the door.

"Yeah. Open the door."

I unhooked the chain and flipped the lock on the knob and opened the door. I was standing there half naked and she looked exactly as she did at the party, except her hair was down. Amazing, like a living dream. I rubbed my face again, making sure I was awake.

Lucy ducked under my arm that was holding the door open. "Sure come in, Lucy," she mimicked my voice.

I looked out the door to see if anyone was with her. There was no one, only tail lights fading out of the gate at the head of the driveway. I closed the door and turned my attention back to her. "Is something wrong?"

Lucy bit her lip and stepped closer to me. "I came to get my birthday present." She reached up and caressed the side of my face.

She didn't have to ask me twice. I scooped her up and she gasped and threw her arms and legs around me. I had an arm around her ass to support her and my hand in her hair as I carried her and sat her on the kitchen bar. I'd wanted to run my hands through her hair and feel it slide between my fingers from the moment I saw her in the back of old Master Pate's truck.

Lucy's breath caught as I sat her down and pulled her to me. I started with her neck and licked a trail from her shoulder to her earlobe. Chill bumps sprang up on her and I could feel her heart rate quicken as I ran my tongue over her neck. Suddenly Lucy snatched back, cupped my face in her hands and planted her lips on mine. The intensity was wild. I was hard and aching for her, the kiss was deeper than anything I'd ever experienced before.

"Lucy, we've got to slow down," I panted as she moved to my Adam's apple and her hands slid down my chest.

"Edward, let me give you something," Lucy said in a breathless whisper. Using her fingertips she found her way to the elastic at the waist of my boxers all the while kissing me.

At first I didn't know what she was talking about and words didn't matter to me right then anyway. I just wanted to kiss her and kiss her and kiss her. I wasn't sure what she had in mind when she slid her hands into the back of my boxers. I just knew I couldn't handle being teased or being her seconds because of what went on with Wilson.

"Lucy," I slipped away, stopping her.

"Edward, please." Lucy reached out for me, but I kept going until I was leaning against the back of the couch.

"What about Wilson Knox?" I asked her.

"What about him?" Lucy's eyes grew wide.

"He broke up with you tonight and now you're here..."

"Oh my God, Edward, you think...Edward, there's only you."

"But..."

"Wilson's gay. He got kicked out of private school because they suspected. He started school with us and the kids were so cruel to him. His family's mean to him. Whitney's mean to everyone, but his whole family acts like they hate him. I asked him out as a cover for him. Nobody thought he was gay anymore once he started dating the homecoming queen. Even his family started treating him differently. I figured of all people who should understand that you can't help who you love, it's me, so I helped him out. That's all there was."

"What about the fight I saw tonight?"

Lucy jumped down off of the bar. "That was staged for everyone to see. Public breakup with a little protest from me sealed it for him."

I shook my head. "You were the homecoming queen? I guess your mother was proud."

Lucy took my hands. "You cannot imagine."

I could see the clock in the kitchen. "It's almost midnight. You should probably get going so you don't miss curfew."

"Maggie dropped me off. My parents think I'm staying at her house." Lucy ran her leg up mine.

"Oh."

What she said a few moments ago replayed in my head. "Edward, I want to give you something." Those words and the fact that she had arranged to stay over, I started to put two and two together.

"I want to wake up next to you again," Lucy all but begged as she wrapped herself around me again.

I found it hard to believe she was here and what she was offering. Lucy offered herself to me once last summer and I'd nearly taken her. In all the months that I struggled to distance myself from her and, with all that went on with Anne, that night played over in my head. I gave her her first orgasm, but I didn't take her virginity. I'd never taken anyone's virginity before. Mainly I didn't take it then because of the age gap between us and the sneaking around we did. Those two things hadn't changed. Lucy was still three years younger than me and this plan of hers to stay over was the epitome of sneaking around. This year I didn't care about those things so much. In this moment with her, they seemed like excuses to perpetuate regret. I had enough regret in my life especially were Lucy was concerned.

"Are you sure, Lucy?"

Her eyes were hooded. She bit her lip and nodded.

"No, you have to say the words." I fisted her hair and pulled her head back to face me. I leaned into her ear, nibbling slightly. "Say the word Lucy and I'm yours."

I could feel her heart rate pick up and her every breath against my chest. "Yes, Edward!"

I lifted her the same as I had when I took her to the kitchen bar, but this time I carried her to my room.

"I'm on the pill." Lucy whispered to me. "It's to regulate things, but I just thought you should know."

"Okay."

At first I thought that was a mood killer for her to mention such a thing, but then it struck me as a turn on. I'd only been with two other girls. One was my first and that was like a science experiment and the other was the Leesburg area's version of Whitney Knox, the town "teacher" of sorts, Beverly Barton. I thought she liked me. I learned a lot from her, like during sex was not the time to try out a hypothesis. I learned as she put it, "To pet the kitty, not beat it." It ended with her as fast as it began.

I'd never had sex with either of those girls without a condom. It was exciting just to think of what that would feel like and to feel it with Lucy made me more erect, which I hardly thought was possible.

I stopped just shy of the bed and Lucy slid her legs down to touch the floor. She stood on her toes, even in the heels, with her arms still draped around my neck and her hands running through my hair. Every follicle I had stood on end. I sealed my lips to hers and pressed in. Our tongues did a rhythmic dance. Every part my body told me to devour her, but good judgement was telling me to slow it down.

I eased back from her. "We can stop whenever you like. All you have to do is say the word."

"Don't stop." Lucy moved my hands to the top of her jeans.

"Shoes first, Green." That was the first time I'd called her 'Green' since I flung the insult toward her that Wednesday night.

I laid her back on the bed and held up her left foot. She put her hands under her head and propped herself up as if watching a show.

"I like these," I said referring to the shoes. They were silver and oozed sex appeal. They sparkled and matched perfectly to the jewelry she had on, bangle earrings and four thin chains around her neck of varying lengths. She looked so much more grown up at this birthday.

"Thank you." Lucy exhaled with a sly smile. The gleam in her eyes sparkled just as brightly as her silver accessories.

I removed the sandal from that foot and then did the same to the other. I massaged each foot after dropping the shoe to the floor. When finished with the shoes, I gripped her behind her knees and pulled her toward the edge. She was light as a ragdoll. I reached for the button on her jeans.

"We don't have to do this," I reminded her while freeing the teeth of her zipper.

"Do you not want to?" she questioned, her voice wavering.

I glanced down at my thin boxers. My body made the answer obvious. Her eyes followed. "I think we both know better than that."

As I slipped her pants down, Lucy had another question. "Have you ever done this before?"

I didn't know whether to be flattered or insulted by the question. If she thought I hadn't, then that meant I was some sort of loser. I mean, what twenty year-old male hadn't lost his virginity this day and age? If she thought I had, well, I didn't want to think of that either.

Despite my reservations, I answered honestly. "Yes. Have you?" I believed I knew the answer, but asked anyway.

"NO!" Clearly off put by the question, Lucy nearly sat up on the bed. The fact that her jeans were caught around her knees made that a little hard. Lucy flopped back down on the bed and regained her composure. "But, I came real close last summer."

My eyes were immediately pulled to hers. I knew the exact moment she was talking about. The memories of that night were hot.

Her legs were free and Lucy was left in nothing, but a pair of black lace panties and her tank top. I'm not sure she was purposefully doing it to drive me wild, but Lucy licked her lips. Seeing her do that, run her tongue across her lips like that, I couldn't take it anymore. She might as well have told me to come hither. Her bottom lip was slightly fuller than her top and they begged for me to make up for time spent not kissing them. Further undressing would come in time.

I eased her legs apart with my knees as I climbed on to the bed and slid between them. She hiked her leg up my side and I could feel the smoothness of her skin graze against my thigh. That touch sent chills up and down my spine. I balanced on one hand and ran the other up that smooth leg of hers. I hovered over her all along, kissing her neck and inching my hand up. Lucy ran her finger tips over my shoulders and more chill bumps sprang up all over my body. I found the trim of her panties and ran a finger around it. I could feel Lucy under me, widening her legs, inviting me, but I didn't go there yet. I continued upward exploring with my hand, finding the hem of her tank top and running my hand under it and around from her side to her back.

"I love your multitasking." Lucy arched her neck offering me better access.

I left her neck and traveled over her shoulder with my tongue. My free hand and my tongue found the spaghetti strap of her tank top on top of her bra strap at the same time. At first I slipped the straps to the side, before deciding it was time for the tank top to disappear. I wanted to see more of her, touch more of her, kiss more of her. I didn't know how much longer I could continue the foreplay, the seduction.

I inched back from her. "Lean up." I quietly requested and she obeyed. "You can still tell me to stop." I offered again.

This time Lucy shook her head, no. I don't know what came over me, but I liked hearing her say the words.

"Out loud, Lucy." I insisted while holding on to the bottom of the tank top, waiting on the word before I took it.

"Don't stop." She put her hands on mine and guided the top upward.

Over her head and flung to the corner of the room it went. Matching black bra, lace, with padding so thin that I could see how perky she was. I had to stop myself from staring. I tried to clear my mind because I wasn't even inside her yet and I was already about to lose control.

Down on the bed we went. I buried my lips in hers. Her taste, a hint of mint, that's what I was thinking when Lucy drew back and bit my bottom lip. My chest pressed to hers and the lace tickled. I thought about that too. Her legs were wrapped around me and the only thing separating us was the material of our underwear, both of which was virtually nonexistent. I could feel the parting of her body as I knew she could feel my length pressing into her. I moved slowly and deliberately, "dry humping" is what Beverly Barton had once called it. Lucy moaned as I moved. That was the sweetest sound I'd ever heard.

I paused to slow the pace. I couldn't go much farther.

"Have I told you how beautiful you are?" I asked her as I ran my hands through her hair and locked eyes with her. "I love your hair like this."

Lucy bit her bottom lip and blushed.

"Clothes on or clothes off, it doesn't matter, you are perfection," I said, admiring her.

Lucy's eyes started to fill with tears.

"What's wrong?" I dabbed my thumb below each eye lid and wiped the tears before they fell.

"Nothing. I think you're more than I could have ever hoped for and I just can't believe you are back. I can't believe you still want me. I thought..."

"I'm so sorry, Lucy. I didn't mean to hurt you. I promise, I'll never do it again. Not ever and you don't have to do this just to keep me." I knew girls back home that thought the only way to keep a guy was to have sex with them.

Lucy pulled me back to her. I kissed her to the point of being drunk with passion. I stripped her from her bra and panties and slipped my boxers down just far enough to free myself. I entered Lucy with a gentle thrust and was met with a gasp.

I withdrew. "Are you okay?" I prayed she was. I was more than okay. I'd never felt anything like it before in my life.

Lucy arched her hips to me. Breathless, "Do it again. Please, do it again, Edward."

I returned my mouth to hers as I gave in to her. Another thrust and another and another. Lucy met me for each. I picked up the pace. I eased back. I was desperate to please her, but I had to admit, "Lucy, I don't know how longer I can last." Lucy was so inexperienced, I'm not sure she entirely knew what I meant.

"I love it when you say my name," she exhaled.

"Lucy." I wanted to add that I loved her, but I didn't want to be that guy that blurted it out during sex. On the other hand, this was more than sex. Sex was what I had with those other girls, this was more.

"Lucy," I said it again.

Her heart rate was increasing with her breathing. "What is this feeling?" she whispered.

There was no time to answer or explain. I could feel her tensing around me. It was the same feeling I'd given her on the floor of the living room in her mother's house on Dixie Drive last summer.

"Oh, God, Edward," Lucy cried out. Pulsating and convulsing, I felt her release so intensely, so much more so than last year. It begged my own release.

We both fell limp afterward. I wrapped her small figure in my arms and cradled her in a spooning position. She was the most precious thing in the world to me. I came to Thomson because I didn't have anywhere else to go. I came to Thomson to win her back and now I had.

I laid there watching Lucy sleep wondering what next. I thought about one of the last conversations with Anne.

"You're going to marry her," Anne told me. She knew it before I did.

Now I had to figure out what to do with my life, how to get back on track and how to pass the time until I could officially make her mine. I'd wanted to be a doctor for as long as I could remember. I wanted it for me and to make my parents proud. I'd worked through all of my schooling with that goal. Now, I wanted to become that for Lucy. I wanted to make a great life for us and to be able to provide for her. We were both so young, but that's what I thought about as I tried to fall asleep next to her.

"I love you, Green," I whispered in her ear. "I'll always love you."

Chapter 12

This morning the sun didn't break through the windows. When it was broad daylight outside, it wasn't broad daylight inside. That was a nice change from the morning before, thanks to the quilts over the window. The nicest change was waking up next to Lucy.

I fell asleep sometime after 2:00 a.m. I'd never slept so soundly in all of my life as I slept that night. There were no dreams or nightmares of Anne. It wasn't a first, but it was a relief. The dreams of Anne, sweet memories that played out on the backs of my eyelids, left me shaken when I awoke as much as the horrifying nightmares or that wicked game of hide and seek in the field did. I had other nights when I didn't dream of her, but those were nights that I basically stayed awake and didn't sleep.

This night was filled with the kind of sleep I had before that dreadful December night. Just holding Lucy in my arms like a child held a stuffed animal brought security and peace. I'm not sure if I would have awoken that morning had Lucy not began to stir in my arms.

Lucy rolled over and nuzzled her nose into my neck. "Good morning," she yawned.

"Good morning," I sighed.

Still trying to get the sleep out of her eyes, Lucy batted her lashes and smiled at me. She stretched, arching her back, and giving a full frontal rub up my chest with her own. During the night the covers had drifted down the bed and we were only covered from the waist down. Lucy's smile was immediately followed by startled look on her face. She realized she was still naked from the night before. She snatched up the covers to shield herself.

"Are you alright?"

Lucy bit her lip, not the same as that come hither kind of biting it that she did last night, but the kind that signified complete and total embarrassment. She closed her eyes and nodded her head.

"You're okay this morning. No regrets?"

She shook her head and answered shyly. "No."

"Are you sure?"

"Yes." There was a little more assurance in her voice.

"But you don't want me to see you naked now?" I paused assessing the condition of the sheets and the distance she'd put between us in the bed. "And you realized..."

Lucy cut me off, "I know but no one's ever seen me naked before."

"Oh."

"What do you mean, 'Oh'?"

I eased toward her side of the bed. I gently pulled back the sheet and Lucy let me, but not without concern. I eased over on top of her propping up on my elbows. "I mean, I'm glad I'm the only one that's ever really seen you."

Lucy slid her fingers through my hair and ran her legs up my sides. It reminded me of last night and I tried hard not to become aroused, but I was already there when I woke up next to her.

"No regrets, you promise me?"

"I promise."

I planted a firm kiss on her lips. I lingered thirty seconds or more before pulling back. "Your lips are so soft."

Lucy had a far-away look in her eyes. "I love kissing you and for a while I thought I might not ever get to kiss you again." She held her breath before confessing, "You broke my heart."

I caressed her cheek with the tip of my nose. "I can't tell you enough that I'm so sorry about that and I'll make you a promise too. I promise I won't ever push you away again."

The moment passed and Lucy changed the subject. "Maggie says I shouldn't have gotten that feeling last summer."

"What feeling is that?"

"You know. *That* feeling." Lucy moved her pelvis against me. "She said I shouldn't get *that* feeling my first time either and some women never get it."

I held back laughing. Sometimes Lucy couldn't help but remind me she was green. "And I assume you like *that* feeling as you call it."

Lucy blushed.

"Can I assume that's a 'yes'? And maybe you'd like it again?"

Lucy drug her nails up my sides. It tickled, but gave me the answer I'd hoped.

I had one more question in between the kisses I planted around her neck traveling down her collarbone. "What time will Maggie be back for you this morning?"

"9:30." Lucy replied with a moan.

That gave me plenty of time to give her "that feeling" as she described it. As Lucy came down off of her high associated with it, she told me more of Maggie's comments on the subject. I inferred that Maggie was quite a bit more experienced in the matter than Lucy.

"She said I should thank my lucky stars you're so talented." Lucy could hardly say it without embarrassment shining through in the form of a red face and giggling.

I found myself a touch embarrassed at that point. Never would I have ever considered myself talented in bed. Thanks to my brief time with Beverly, the word "trained" might have been a better description. I didn't want to get into that with Lucy so I didn't exactly know how to respond. I rolled onto my back and she snuggled into me, laying her head on my chest.

"Are you and Maggie this open about everything?" I already suspected I knew the answer.

"Yes, I suppose. I mean, don't you have someone you talk about everything with?" Lucy squirmed a little to get comfortable and again pulled at the sheets to make sure she was completely covered.

"Not anymore." I didn't mean to be a buzz kill, but there it was, an inference to Anne. I immediately tried to salvage the mood. "Maybe I've found someone new that I can share everything with."

I kissed Lucy playfully on the top of her head before easing from under her. I exited the bed to the call of nature. I left all covers behind, figuring the best way to make her comfortable in nothing but her skin was to show her that I was comfortable in mine. I wasn't one to prance around naked, but I walked around the bed and through the room to the bathroom as natural as I would had I been clothed. I returned exactly as I had left and Lucy took notice.

"You like?" I teased her.

Busted looking at me, Lucy turned her face away and hid it in a pillow.

"Am I to take it that you didn't enjoy the view?"

Lucy peered up at me covering her smile with both hands.

"Lucy, it's okay to like looking. It doesn't make you a pervert or anything. I like looking, actually, I love looking at you. You're beautiful and most girls would kill to look like you. I'm not telling you to strut around naked all the time, I'm just saying you certainly don't have to be uncomfortable around me."

Lucy nodded. "Mama says modesty is a virtue."

"Your mother is pregnant right now. How do you think she got that way?"

"Fair enough," Lucy replied with exasperation.

Lucy glanced over at the clock. 9:05. "I should probably be getting up."

"What's stopping you?" I made a point of not getting back in the bed with her while the conversation went on.

"Could you hand me my clothes?" Lucy pointed to her jeans that were in a pile near the foot of the bed while trying to divert her eyes from me.

"Do you plan on getting them on while under the covers? And, look at me when I talk to you." I held back the urge to laugh.

She did as I said and her eyes grew wide. Her unspoken question was in the air, "How did you know?" coupled with the fact that she'd never allowed herself to fully look at me until then.

I picked up the jeans as she asked, but held them out, not letting her have them.

"Edward!"

"Come and get them, Lucy!"

Just at that moment a slight nocking came from the door to the apartment.

"Shit!" Lucy exclaimed. As far as I could recall that was the first four letter word I'd ever heard her say. "It's Maggie! She's perpetually early for everything!"

I threw her jeans to her and we both scrambled to get dressed. Another round of knocking and then another as I finished throwing on my shorts. This time I could see my t-shirt and threw it on as I went for the door.

I opened the front door of the apartment and gestured for her to come inside. "Morning, Maggie."

"Morning." Maggie knew full well what had gone on the night before and couldn't look me in the eye at that particular moment.

"Lucy'll be out in a moment."

Maggie passed straight on by me carrying a small duffle bag in her hand and headed for the bedroom door which I had closed on my way out of it. Before entering the room Maggie turned back to me. She walked right up to me and bowed up her petite chest as if she was a man that could match me in a fight if she so chose. "If you ever hurt her again, you'll have me to deal with and you know the reputation us red heads have! Quick tempered and mean as shit, in case you haven't heard."

"O-kay..." I furrowed my brow and decided not to engage further. I knew I'd hurt Lucy in the past and I felt terrible about that. Maggie had every right to be protective of her friend and feel skeptical of me. I didn't see how she could carry out a threat, but I trusted that she wouldn't have to try.

Maggie tapped on the door. "Lucy, it's me. I've got your clothes."

Lucy opened the door fully dressed in her attire from the night before.

"We can't have you going to church this morning in the same outfit you wore last night." Maggie handed her the bag.

Lucy didn't just grab the bag she grabbed Maggie by the wrist and jerked her into the room. The door promptly shut behind them. I busied myself with making a pot of coffee and starting breakfast. The contents of my kitchen were bleak, but I had some frozen waffles and figured that would do.

As I hovered over the toaster oven, I could make out very little of their conversation. I wasn't trying to listen, but occasionally I could hear my name and I heard a great deal of giggling.

When the girls finally emerged from the room, I offered each of them a plate of waffles and a cup of coffee. Now they were both dressed for church, but unlike Maggie who appeared on her way to a country bar, Lucy was conservative with her dress and makeup. She was flawless. I handed them their plates at the bar and kept my stance on the other side. I had trouble keeping my hormones in check just looking at her. The last thing I needed was giving Maggie more of a show than I already did by wearing just my boxers to the door.

Maggie glanced at Lucy, "And he cooks too." She fanned herself for a moment before her attention turned back to me. "Wipe that smile off your face. I still mean what I said a few minutes ago. Don't make me hurt you!"

Most of the time when folks joke they give some sort of indication, a wink, a slight chuckle, something. Not Maggie. I couldn't tell whether she was joking or not. I figured I'd stick with my original plan to avoid hurting Lucy in the future and then I wouldn't have to find out if her little red haired friend was completely crazy.

The girls scarfed down the breakfast as fast as they could. There was some small talk over breakfast, but mainly the girls just scarfed it down.

"I'll wait in the car," Maggie said as she gathered the bag she'd brought in for Lucy.

I pulled Lucy into my arms. I fought the urge to tell her I loved her. I still didn't want it to be the consolation prize for her virginity. The two were mutually exclusive of one another and I didn't want them intertwined.

Lucy cupped my cheek in her hand. Hers was the softest touch I'd ever felt. I'd not just slept with her, I'd slept beside her. I would have given anything to have made that a ritual, sleeping next to her, waking up next to her.

I brushed an errant hair from her face and tucked it behind her ear. "What are you doing this afternoon?" I asked.

"After church me and Lily and Daddy will probably go to White Columns for lunch, but after that... Well, there's the hunt this afternoon."

"How would you feel if I met you all for lunch?"

A light danced in her eyes and before she answered, I already knew it was a "yes."

"Perfect. There's something I need to ask your father."

Lucy grew curious. "What?"

"That's for me to know and for you to find out," I teased her.

Lucy shook her head. "Have I ever told you that I don't particularly like surprises?"

"Have I ever told you that I really like to kiss you?"

Lucy's face flushed and she looked away.

"Oh, no, Lucy Meeks, don't look away." I raised her chin with my fingers and sealed her mouth with mine.

Gently, I explored her mouth as Lucy held tight around my neck. I could have gone on for hours, but I needed to let her go. I wouldn't dare have her be late to church and risk our perfect night together being discovered. I didn't want to ruin it for either of us.

I eased back from our embrace. "Go on. Get!" I whirled Lucy around and aimed her toward the door.

She squealed with amusement. Lucy stopped just inside the threshold of the door and turned back to me. "Hey, Edward."

"Yes, Lucy?"

"Thank you for last night and for this morning."

"No. Thank you."

"Okay. White Columns at 12:30. Be there. I'll save you a seat next to me." Lucy blew me a kiss and then out the door she went.

Chapter 13

12:25 p.m. I was early. I stood on the porch of White Columns Inn admiring the bluest skies I could recall in recent memory. There wasn't a cloud to be seen and, regardless of the weather, it was already shaping up to be the best day I'd had in a while.

White Columns was the nicest hotel in Thomson. It was out by the interstate and not terribly far from the hunt club. The thing it was most known for wasn't the rooms or the rates. It was known for the lunch buffet that the restaurant put on. They had the best fried chicken and I remembered it well from last summer. People came from as far as three counties over just to relive Sunday lunch at their grandmother's table.

I stood on the brick porch between the columns as many of the churchgoers started to file in. Mr. Watson wasn't the only member of the hunt who liked to be a part of the Sunday lunch crowd at White Columns. At least a dozen other members passed by me on their way in and stopped to hug me, pat my back or shake my hand. They were all well-meaning and they helped to calm my nerves. I was there with a purpose and it wasn't just to have lunch with Lucy and her family.

All morning, I replayed my night with Lucy. I still couldn't wrap my mind around how beautiful she was and that she'd let me back into her life.

I remembered tracing a line down her skin from her neck to her thigh as she laid on her side, trying to regain control of her breathing. The flat sheet of the bed was thrown down to just above her knee and drawn up her front, gripped in her hands.

"I never forgot one detail of you and I never will. It was thoughts of you that kept me going the last six months." I buried my face in her hair. "If I died tomorrow, I would die complete. You are my Helen of Troy."

Lucy didn't say a word. I don't know if she heard me or not. I figured she was asleep.

I knew the activities like those of last night would have to be kept from her parents, but I still didn't want to sneak around like we did last year. I wanted to be able to date her openly. I wanted to put my hand on the small of her back and lead her into a room without wondering if anyone would notice. I wanted to kiss her without worrying that someone would see and tell. I wanted to be able to let the world know that I was hers.

I dressed as if I'd been to church, but I hadn't. I even put on the one tie that I brought with me from Virginia. I owned more ties, but I didn't figured there'd be much of a need for them in my foreseeable future. Most days all I needed was a pair of jeans and a t-shirt, but today I figured I needed a little more. I needed to be at my best. White button down shirt, khaki slacks and the baby blue checked tie that my mother bought for me that she said brought out the color of my eyes. That's what I was wearing.

Ten minutes later than I expected I finally saw Mr. Watson's Mercedes pull into the parking lot. Lily was in the front seat so I couldn't see Lucy until the car turned into a space. I loved the way her face lit up at the sight of me so much that I could not have contained the smile on my face if I'd tried. Lucy waved when she stepped out of the car and I waved back.

I intended to watch Lucy as she made the walk to me, but Mr. and Mrs. Williams from the club approached from the side.

"Edward," Mr. Williams called my name and redirected my attention. He stuck out his hand for a shake. "Are we still on for this afternoon?"

"As far as I know we are." My voice elevated to a higher pitch in reaction to the pain. Mr. Williams might have been a gray haired man nearing eighty, but he had the strength of a young athlete.

"Well, I look forward to it," Mr. Williams said as he relinquished my hand.

Mrs. Williams, not nearly as old as her husband, probably thirty years younger to be honest, leaned in for a hug and extended an invitation. "Why don't you join us for lunch?"

"Thank you so much, but I'm meeting the Watson's and here they are." I motioned toward Lucy and Lily and Mr. Watson who were now on the steps.

"Cliff," Mr. Watson said acknowledging Mr. Williams.

"Boyd," Mr. Williams reciprocated and he stuck out his hand to Mr. Watson. It crossed my mind to try to warn Mr. Watson, but what would I say? Plus, I really didn't want him to think I was a wimp, hurt by a little hand shake.

"Come on, Cliff, I am famished. Y'all can chat in the woods this afternoon," Mrs. Williams tugged at her husband's coat sleeve.

"Allison," Mr. Watson spoke to her as well. "Good to see you."

Lucy and Lily remained silent, listening to the greetings. It appeared to me that Lucy could no more keep her eyes off of me than I could keep mine off of her.

Mr. Williams gave me a razzing punch in the arm. "She gets mean when she gets hungry." Mr. Williams then held the door for his wife and they went on inside.

"Good afternoon, sir." I extended my hand to Mr. Watson.

Refuting my offer, Mr. Watson threw his arm around me in a side hug. "I think I've had about all of the handshakes I can muster. I thought Cliff was going to take me to my knees then."

I was relieved it wasn't just me. "I know exactly what you mean." I wiggled the fingers on my right hand.

When Mr. Watson released me I stepped ahead to get the door for the girls.

"Lucy tells me she invited you to lunch with us today."

Lucy winked at me as she went in and Lily thanked me for getting the door as she passed by.

"Thanks for having me," I replied to Mr. Watson as he entered behind his daughters.

"Anytime."

The hostess showed the four of us to a square table in the back corner. I pulled out the chair for Lucy and Mr. Watson did the same for Lily. Once we were seated the waitress took our drink order the girls went to make their plates at the buffet.

I watched Lucy and admired her figure. She was lovely and every head in the room turned as she walked by. Her dress was flowing and hung about four inches above her knees. It was the same one she had on after her shower and darted out of my apartment earlier, but I hadn't given it much thought then. I was still stuck with the image of her lying naked in my bed. It occurred to me then that I'd never seen her in a dress before. I'd seen Lily in plenty of dresses. They were a staple of her wardrobe, but not Lucy's.

I was on a mission to ask Mr. Watson if I could date Lucy and I knew there'd never be a more opportune time to ask, but it took me a moment to break my focus on Lucy's legs. They were tan and long and muscular. The memory of my fingers gliding up them, how smooth they were, was fresh on in my mind. I nearly got hard just thinking about them and watching her walk through the restaurant.

Mr. Watson was content to make small talk about the heavenly smell of fried chicken that filled the room. I didn't want to talk about chicken, but I had trouble working up the courage to spit out my question. I needed to stick to my agenda.

I plotted all morning just what I'd say, but when I opened my mouth none of what I rehearsed came out. "Mr. Watson, umm," I stuttered through his name and lost my train of thought. I started again, "Sir, uhhh..."

I took a sip of water as Mr. Watson stared at me.

"Are you alright, son?" He asked a legitimate question considering I'd never been tongue tied in front of him before.

I cleared my throat and started for the third time. "Mr. Watson, would you mind if I asked Lucy out?"

"Good Lord, boy, I was getting worried you were trying to ask for her hand in marriage. You can imagine my relief."

My face flashed red. I knew if she was older than seventeen and I had a dime to my name to buy a ring and that would have been exactly what I was doing.

Mr. Watson fidgeted, straightening his silverware as I waited. He was clearly contemplating his answer and that bothered me. Of course, I had hoped for a straight forward "yes."

Mr. Watson leaned across the table as not to have the entire church congregation hear our conversation. "Look. Here's the thing; I know about last year with you and Lucy. To put it plainly, you broke her heart. Now, I know as well as the next father that teenage girls are bound to get their hearts broken. It's a part of growing up, but does that mean I want it to happen? No."

"I know, sir, and I'm real sorry about that..."

"Let me finish," he insisted. "I'm sure you are sorry especially now that you are back down here. I'm also sure that Lucy represents stability and familiarity for you and based on what your mother told me about what happened to your sister, I know you are probably craving those things right now. I feel for you, I do, but do you think it's fair for Lucy to get involved with you again knowing that you're

147

going to have to leave for school in another two months?"

Mother might have told him about Anne, but she didn't tell him the whole story. She didn't tell him that I wasn't going back to school. I figured there was no time like the present to address that detail.

"That's the other thing I was hoping to ask you about," I began.

"What's that?" Mr. Watson was confused.

"I wanted to talk to you about staying on at the hunt club."

"What about your college?" he asked with his head cocked and his voice full of concern.

"I filled out an application for admission to Augusta State this week and I'm going to talk to the bank here in Thomson about a student loan." I also explained to him why I could not go back to school at Thomas Jackson and that my father cut me off.

Mr. Watson leaned back in his chair, pondering all that I had said. "Ah," was his only comment.

The girls were held up at the buffet line by several ladies asking about Lucy's mother and how her pregnancy was going. The stretch of silence in my conversation with Mr. Watson allowed me to eaves drop on the girls for a moment.

Eventually Mr. Watson called my attention back to him. "Do you still plan on going to medical school?"

Mr. Watson paused for the waitress to deliver our drinks. "Thank you," we both said to her.

I answered his question. "I don't know how much hope there is for me to become a doctor at the

148

rate things are going. With my father cutting me off and now I'm going to have to finance the rest of my undergrad degree, it makes me nervous about coming out of school with so much debt that there's no hope of ever paying it all off."

Mr. Watson continued. "Do you remember the first time your father introduced you to me?"

"No, sir."

"He said, 'This is my son, Edward. He thinks he's going to be a doctor one day.' The way he said it got under my skin. I won't go into the specifics. Let's just say I didn't share the love of your father that some of the other members of the hunt had. I believe parents should believe in their children so that the children will believe in themselves. You understand what I'm saying?"

"I think so." Honestly, I wasn't real sure what he was getting at, but luckily he went on.

"Now's not the time to give up on that dream. If you give up he'll win," Mr. Watson pointed out.

"I'd like to pay my way as I went, but I just don't know if that's possible right now. You already don't like him so it won't do much harm in telling you that he cleaned out my bank account. When I was a child my parents set up an account for me. Every dime I made and any money that anyone ever gave me was put in that account. Because it was set up when I was a child, it had to have one of my parents' names on it. His name was on the account with mine and as a way of punishing me for what happened with Anne, he emptied my account. There was enough that I could have paid for my last two years of school. So, now you see why I have to get a loan."

Mr. Watson just shook his head in disgust. "I'll write him a letter on Monday as your attorney and I'll see that you get your money back."

"I can't ask you to do that."

"You're not asking. I'm offering." Mr. Watson took a swig of his sweet tea. "Regardless of getting the money back, there's something I want you to consider."

"Anything," I was so grateful I'd have agreed to almost anything.

"I want you to consider talking to a recruiter with the Navy," Mr. Watson suggested.

"Okay?" That's not what I expected him to say.

Mr. Watson went on to describe the benefits of service. "You could make money while you are serving and they will pay for your education. That solves the whole problem with your finances and your education. I had a buddy that went into the Navy right after high school. He didn't come from parents who had money to pay for his college. His education, including law school, was on Uncle Sam's dime. He's now a lawyer same as me. A doctor's a doctor, son, it doesn't matter how you get there as long as you get there."

It was definitely something to consider and I'd never thought of it before. I'd never had anyone take an interest in me enough to guide me and give me good advice.

"Another bonus is that you could use the Navy to go overseas to visit your mother. Would you be able to afford to do that while attending Augusta State and working at the hunt barn?"

"No, sir. I guess not."

"Seriously, son, I think telling you to talk to a recruiter is about the best advice I can give you."

"Yes, sir." I then agreed to think about it. I also wanted to talk to Lucy about such an idea.

The girls finally returned with their plates Mr. Watson and I excused ourselves to the buffet to make our own plates before we all continued with lunch. Mr. Watson never said anything more about me dating Lucy while we ate and he didn't mention a word about our conversation. I really wanted an answer, but I didn't want to press him. I didn't know what I was going to do if he didn't give his approval and the wait was killing me.

The most significant conversation while we ate was that of them letting me know that they'd broken the news about Anne to Lily. Lily said what everyone said when they found out. "I'm so sorry about your loss. She was so sweet."

Lily's eyes filled with tears and Mr. Watson promptly changed the subject.

"Looks like it might be clouding up out there." Mr. Watson directed us toward the nearest window.

Lucy nudged me under the table. "I hope it doesn't affect our chances to hunt this afternoon."

"I hope not too," added Lily as she took another bite of her chicken.

Lily's appetite had sure increased from last year. I looked at her plate thinking about how she'd eaten as much as I had.

"Are you thinking of joining us today?" Mr. Watson asked Lily.

"I was thinking of riding in the truck with Big Daddy so Lucy could ride in the field," Lily replied. "I know Blueberry's out of commission right now;

but I'm sure she can borrow a horse from someone at the hunt barn. Plus, you promised last month that she could ride with the whips and she hasn't been able to for having to get the gates for Big Daddy and I can get the gates."

Big Daddy was what most of the younger generation called old Master Pate. From what I gathered he was like another grandfather for most of them like Lily.

"I think I could be persuaded to be alright with that." Mr. Watson gave Lily a nod of his head and a smile. I had the sneaking suspicion Lucy and Lily had concocted a plan to allow Lucy and I some alone time. Mr. Watson was no fool.

"As long as I'm not the whip that has to ride with Lucy. I don't want her slowing me up if we get on the scent of a fox."

"I'm sure Edward wouldn't mind if I tagged along with him," Lucy chimed in.

"Edward, what do you say?" Lily smiled.

"Well, I don't want her slowing me down either," I joked.

Lucy gave me a swat on the arm. "I'm sure I can ride as well and as fast as either of you."

"You wish!" Mr. Watson playfully snapped at her. "You're going to have to persuade Edward."

Mr. Watson gave me a wink and I think that was my answer as to whether I could date Lucy. I didn't think for a moment that he gave in at my request. He didn't give in at my request. He gave in because it was what Lucy wanted and that was evidenced by hers and Lily's plotting.

Chapter 14

Clouds started rolling in while we were at lunch and continued to build all afternoon. We watched the radars and the sky and the rain wasn't due until later that evening. No rain meant the hunt would go on as scheduled. No rain meant I'd get to spend time with Lucy and I could not get enough of that.

Members started trailering in horses as early as 1:30 p.m. but I didn't go out until I saw Mr. Watson's car turn down the driveway. I spent the time daydreaming about my night with Lucy and thinking about what Mr. Watson said about the Navy. I had to admit to myself that it wasn't a bad idea. The real problem I saw with it was that I'd have to be away from Lucy a lot. I hated the thought of leaving her. Regardless of the decision I had to make, I decided I would talk to her about it first. I knew it directly affected my immediate future, but I liked to think it would affect her future as well.

We never turned the hounds loose on Sunday afternoons until 4:00 p.m., but by 3:30 all of the trailers were in, horses were unloaded and saddled. Mrs. Harper loaned me the beast again and I was adjusting his saddle in the yard of the barn when I spotted Lucy. She was saddling up a one of Master Pate's fillies. Seeing her bend over in her hunt attire sent my mind straight to the gutter. No one wore the tan stretch pants that were a part of the uniform better. They hugged the curve of her ass so well that it left me praying I would have her alone soon. Since last year, Lucy had filled out in all the right places.

The horse suited Lucy. It was the prettiest of the hunt just like the girl set to ride it. It was a paint named Oreo due to her markings.

As discussed at lunch, Lucy went out with the whips instead of the field. By her father's suggestion, she was paired with me. Lily volunteered to ride with old Master Pate and he was eager to have the company.

While milling around waiting to get started Mr. Williams strode up to me. I didn't let him get to close, but it was quite the conversation.

"You know he's nearly ninety and still quite a rounder. If he dies back in the woods with one of these girls, you know what the rumor will be?"

I knew what Mr. Williams was suggesting and I didn't like it much. "Excuse me?"

"They'll say he died getting it on with them in the woods."

I shook my head and was relieved that Mrs. Harper's mule headed animal started to bite at Mr. Williams' horse. That made it easy to get away from him without letting him know how unamused I was by his insinuations.

The animal had a name, Pats Blue Ribbon, kind of like the beer, but not quite. Mrs. Harper referred to him as PBR. To me, he was Beastly due to his demeanor. As it turned out I wasn't the only one that felt the need to impress a girl. Lucy brought Oreo up next to us and Beastly didn't budge. I doubted how long he could contain himself since the whole reason Mrs. Harper had him boarded at the hunt barn was because he could not get along with any of her other horses. He struggled with the horses at the hunt barn as well.

When the hounds were turned loose and took off, Lucy gave Oreo the command to go and she went. Beastly fell in behind her as soon as I gave him a tap with the back of my heel. With ease we caught up to Lucy. While Master Pate took the hounds through the property behind the hunt barn, Lucy and I took the left flank and went into the field that bordered the road. Her father and Mr. Williams took the right flank.

At the far back of the field, near the tree line, Lucy rode Oreo ahead of me and then brought her around. The walkie-talkies were filled with chatter, but the hounds had not struck a scent yet and we were far enough away that we didn't even hear them in the distance. We were quite alone.

I stopped my horse to see what Lucy was doing. She sucked her teeth and gave the reins another gentle tug, bringing Oreo up so close to Beastly that the only thing keeping their bellies from rubbing against one another was our boots in the stirrups.

"I'd be careful," I warned her. "I don't call him 'Beast' for nothing." I patted him on the neck. "He's damn near wild."

"He's fine. Now lean over here." Lucy bit her bottom lip. She took me by the lapel on my jacket and pulled me toward her.

My top lip touched hers first followed by my nose, I tilted at an angle to access her mouth. Her tongue tasted like grape bubble gum and moved like warm silk against mine. Her gloved hand was gripped around the back of my neck and held me tight. I was no limp fish, but Lucy was the driving force behind this kiss. Dressed in a long sleeve jacket, long pants and boots on a ninety degree day, she gave me chills. This was the most erotic thing I'd ever done on a horse.

"That was for speaking to Daddy and asking to date me." Lucy wasn't finished. "And this," she ran her index finger around my collar and hooked her finger inside my shirt, pulling me back by the spot where my top button came together. "This is to thank you for last night."

"No, thank *you*," I corrected her just before she sealed our lips together again.

Beastly stayed still as a stone, but twenty or thirty seconds more of toe curling kissing and Oreo shifted her weight. It caused Lucy to lose her balance and down between the two horses she started. I grabbed for her and got a good hold, but, in her scrambling, Lucy gave Oreo a heel to the side, the signal to move.

Both Lucy and I screamed, "Whoa!" at the same time, but Lucy added in terror, "Edward, my boot is caught!"

Her boot was caught in the stirrup. I held tight to her, but there'd have been nothing I could do if Oreo had taken off. I would have lost my grip and Lucy would have been drug along.

Oreo didn't break for it, but she was definitely moving. Both of us knew what could happen and I'm not sure who was more scared.

Thinking fast, I shouted, "Grab for the saddle horn!" And with all my strength I threw Lucy up and in the direction of the saddle. It was the only hope I had in case Oreo didn't stop.

As soon as I let go of her, and without taking my eyes off of her, I jerked the reins of my horse and turned to follow.

Oreo took a few more quick steps, picking up speed, and Lucy screamed, "Oh my God! WHOA!" as she clawed her way back up. Lucy made her way back to the saddle just as Oreo started to run, but, luckily, Oreo heeded her cries and stopped.

By the time I reached her, Lucy was in tears, but she was fine. I'd never been so relieved of anything in my entire life. I jumped down and grabbed both horses by the lead, effectively keeping either from making a move without my permission.

"Are you okay?" I'm not sure I was able to cover the fact that I was still shaking. It might have shown in my question.

"It just scared me, that's all." Lucy nodded as she reassured me.

I let out a sigh of relief, but I couldn't speak.

"Are you okay?" She wiped her eyes and looked down at me again. "You're white as a ghost."

"I'm fine if you're fine."

Being drug was every rider's worst fear. Everyone feared being thrown, but, injured or not, the outcome was the same, the rider was free from the horse. Being drug was the opposite. You weren't free at all. You were caught, stuck and virtually helpless.

What was worse than the thought of me being drug? Worse was the thought of it happening to Lucy. It happened so fast and she wasn't hurt, but it could have ended so differently. It could have really hurt her or killed her. My worst fears, that I didn't

157

even know I had until that moment, were nearly realized.

"Jump down for a moment." My voice wasn't shaking anymore. In that moment, I knew I had to tell her. I had to say it out loud.

Lucy stayed put. "I'm fine. Really."

"Please get down. I have to tell you something and I'd rather do it eye to eye."

Lucy slung her leg around. She slid down and I caught her, wrapping her in my arms.

Lucy's eyes were piercing, more so now than ever. I swear she could see all the way to my soul and she was searching me for a clue as to what I was about to tell her. The wind picked up and blew her hair across her face. I rounded up the strays and twirled the strands of hair around my finger.

"I love you, Lucy Meeks. I've loved you since I first laid eyes on you. Waking up next to you this morning was the highlight of my life."

There was a pause. I suppose I expected her to say it in reciprocation, but I really didn't care whether she said it or not. I just needed her to know how I felt about her.

I hadn't paid any attention to the noises from the walkie-talkie since Lucy first kissed me. Our eyes were locked and I was just about to kiss her again when I heard the yell, "Tally-Ho!" That would get even the most distracted fox hunter's attention. Tally-Ho, translation, they'd spotted a fox. It was basically a battle cry. It was blaring through the speaker and coming from a voice through the singing of the hounds. They were coming our way and a fox had been sighted.

Lucy and I moved fast. I hoisted her onto Oreo and I threw a leg up into Beastly's stirrup and away we went toward the action. No trotting, no cantering, we had the horses at a full sprint. We fell in with the other riders in pursuit of the hounds. Tearing through the woods, ducking limbs, dodging branches and jumping fallen trees, it lasted an hour or more. Of the two of us, Lucy led and she'd come so far in her riding since that first lesson last year. We'd come so far since that first lesson.

The hounds caught the fox that afternoon and as I held Oreo's reigns, Lucy mixed drinks in the back of old Master Pate's truck again. Soon enough the hunt was over, the horses and hounds were put up and Lucy and I were the last ones left at the club. I took a seat at the top of the stairs outside of the apartment door. That was my front porch and it allowed me a view of the ring where I gave Lucy her first riding lesson. There were many moments in the past few weeks where I sat in that spot and watched the memory of that meeting play out in front of me like a movie. I patted a spot next to me, instructing Lucy to have a seat.

Lucy flopped down next to me so close that our legs touched from the hip to the knee and down to our ankles. I casually slung an arm over her knee and she leaned her head against my shoulder. I was content to sit in silence with her and watch the sun set and for a while, there were no words to describe the peace I felt just being with her.

I'm not sure how much time passed, but, barely above a whisper I heard her say it. "I love you, too."

I turned my face to her and she lifted her head. Her eyes were full of tears and one was just about to slip free. With the pad of my thumb, I wiped it gently from just below her eye lid.

"I'm sorry I didn't say it immediately. I just, well, I've never been in love before and I haven't had the best example and I didn't think... Well, I knew I loved you, but to hear you tell me, I was stunned. I hoped you did, but..."

I stopped her. "Of course I love you. I never want you to doubt that again. I'll probably be yours until long after you don't want me anymore." I shrugged my shoulders and smiled at her before pulling her into my arms.

I had to keep reminding myself that she was only seventeen. As much as I wanted her to, I knew she couldn't live, breath, sleep and wake up with me every morning. The freedom to be like that with her was likely years away.

"Lucy, you scared the life out of me when you almost fell off of the horse this afternoon. I cannot bear the thought of losing you." The image of Anne flashed through my mind. This had been the longest I'd gone without thinking of her since I lost her. "I don't know what I'd do if I lost you, too."

"I'm fine now and you saved me. I'm yours and I'm pretty sure you're not going to lose me." Lucy's eyes brightened. "I'm serious, I love you to the moon and back Edward Stephens."

We sat watching the shade fall over the pasture from the barn as the sun set behind us. Our hands were clasped together with our fingers interlocked. Lucy laid her head back on my shoulder. I wanted to take her to bed again, but I let the urge pass. As much as I wanted to experience her body intertwined with mine again, I didn't want that to become all we did together.

Time passed and July was suddenly upon us. Lucy and I spent every possible moment together. We went to dinner and to the movies. We had her friends over to the apartment for cook outs and Maggie made fun of us for becoming an old married couple. If that's what we were, I was fine with it and it suited us. As much as we went out, we stayed in and that's what we enjoyed the most. The best times were those when we were just sitting on the top step, my little porch, watching the sun set and talking.

One such night leading up to the 4th, Lucy and I sat on the porch with her head resting softly on my shoulder when she sighed, "What am I going to do when you go back home at the end of the summer?"

Both of us had avoided the topic of me leaving. I avoided it because I had no home to go back to and I hadn't been able to nail down my plans of what to do next. I hadn't heard back regarding my application to Augusta College. I knew it was a stretch to get accepted due to my application being late, but I wasn't thrilled with the alternative that Mr. Watson suggested. It made perfect sense for my financial future, but joining the Navy would take me away from Lucy and the thought of leaving her made me physically ill.

I think Lucy avoided the topic with the notion that if we didn't talk about it then it wouldn't happen. As long as we didn't say I was leaving, maybe I wasn't. I think both of us avoided the topic for fear of ruining what time we had with thoughts of the end.

With Lucy asking the question she did, it made me feel the need to address it, to tell her my circumstances. I started the conversation by asking her, "How would you feel about me staying on here in Thomson?"

Lucy whipped around to face me. Her smile was wide with excitement over the initial prospect of me staying, but her sensibilities quickly took over. "What about your college?" Dropping the smile, she crossed her top teeth behind her bottom ones and curled her nose like she smelled something.

"I've applied to Augusta State, but I haven't heard back yet."

"What does your family think of you staying down here?"

"My mother is coming here in a week," I explained.

Mother had put off the trip a couple of times, but this time she promised she wasn't changing.

I continued "You can ask her yourself..."

"What? You're mother's coming and this is the first I'm hearing of it?" She rung her hands and fidgeted. Her voice was caught between excitement and nervousness.

"Yes, my mother is stopping by for a visit before flying out to England. She's moving to England to live with her family and my sister, B. I thought I told you."

"No. You didn't tell me." Lucy punched me in the arm. "I have got a million things to do. Oh my God, I've got to clean the apartment and..."

"Lucy, seriously, I'll take care of everything. She's going to love you and you don't have to do anything, but be yourself."

Clearly her mind was racing in a million directions. "I can't believe you're just telling me this. What about your father?"

Lucy shook her head and tiny strands of her hair fell from the messy bun she'd pulled it into for work earlier in the day. I could hardly think from being distracted just looking at her. Nervous, was a good look on her.

"Come here," I said as I pulled her over into a position in my lap, straddling me.

Lucy draped her arms over my shoulders and we were face to face. I nuzzled into her neck, planting featherlike kisses on her skin. She still smelled of the kennel and I smelled of the horse barn, but neither of us complained.

"Seriously, Edward."

"My father cut me off and we're pretty much dead to one another." There was nothing sweet about it so I kept up my efforts to distract Lucy.

"That's terrible!"

"It is what it is. He blames me for Anne and I know I've told you that before."

"Yes, yes."

"Yes, yes, keep going," I asked as I unbuttoned the top two buttons of her shirt. "Or, yes, yes, you understand? I prefer the first."

"Edward!"

"What time do you have to be home tonight?" I fisted the knot of her hair and arched her head back allowing me access to the void where those open buttons had been. "Cleavage, umm, I love it." I moaned as I ran my tongue between her breasts.

"No changing the subject." She squirmed, but I didn't let go.

"Come on, I don't want talk of my father to spoil the night."

"Nothing could spoil the night, except you refusing to talk."

I let out a heavy breath and rolled my eyes. I thought for a moment before suggesting a compromise. "I'll tell you everything you want to know, if you'll call Maggie and have her cover for you tonight."

Lucy hadn't slept over since the night of her birthday party. We'd made love a number of times since then, but she hadn't stayed over and I was dying to wake up with her again.

"Fine."

Lucy made the call and Maggie agreed. She'd do anything for Lucy and I envied that kind of friendship. My father never allowed us away from him long enough to make friendships like that. I know now that keeping us close kept him in control.

Chapter 15

We dropped Lucy's car off at Maggie's and then headed across town to get dinner. Lucy wanted a chocolate milkshake and she said I hadn't lived until I had one from Kent's.

"It's a Thomson institution. It's no theme park, but it's to Thomson what Six Flags is to Atlanta, where everyone goes in the summers. Honestly, you should be glad you have me to turn you on to these things."

"Oh, Lucy, honey," I inched the hand that wasn't on the steering wheel up her inner thigh toward the hem of her shorts. "I am so glad I have you to turn me on."

Lucy playfully slapped my hand. "Focus on the road, please."

"I could turn around and focus on you at home."

"Patience. I really want my milkshake."

"This better be a good milkshake."

"It's the best! Totally worth waiting for."

"Really?" I teased her by running my thumb just under the hem of her shorts.

Lucy squirmed in the passenger's seat. "The road. Please."

Feeling her whip around in the seat, I cut my eyes at her to see her facing out the side window. I didn't think we still had boundaries, but feared I might have crossed a line. I snatched back my hand. "Sorry."

"What?"

I glanced at her again. She looked like she'd seen a ghost and there was a tremor to her voice. The drain of her color caused me to slow the truck. "Are you okay?"

Lucy glanced behind us, down the road, once more and looked back before she answered. "Ya...yes." She never stuttered, but she did then and I was not convinced of her answer.

"Are you sure?" I checked the review mirror to see if I could see what spooked her. I didn't see anything out of the ordinary. A small red truck, a blue sedan, a white, two silver and one brown car that someone probably bought thinking it was Champagne, but it was definitely brown.

Lucy attempted to shake off whatever it was that had rattled her. "It was nothing." She switched gears. "Get in the turning lane," she pointed toward the lane leading up to the red light at Hill Street.

"Okay, but you know you can tell me what's wrong."

"I'm fine. I mean it." Lucy took my hand and kissed the back of it before putting it back on her leg.

It wasn't long before we pulled into the driveway at Kent's and Lucy bounced out of the Bronco like nothing was wrong. She beat me to the front and grabbed my hand. Her palm was still a touch damp even though I noticed her wipe her hands on her pants not too long after she assured me she was alright. It ate at me that she wouldn't tell me what was wrong, but I didn't push her. She ordered for the both of us and she was right.

"This is the best milkshake I've ever had," I told Lucy as I slurped the last bit through the straw.

Lucy didn't hear me. "Huh?"

I put my cup down and demanded Lucy's attention by taking her hands in mine. "Okay, it's time to tell me what you saw and I mean be honest. Don't tell me it's nothing."

"I thought I saw someone, but it's not possible. It really was nothing." She looked at me adoringly as she spoke. She smiled with the perfect amount of teeth showing, batted her eyes just enough and tilted her head with a forward nod. She could have sold me the Golden Gate Bridge while I forgot my own name just with that look. She stole my mind in that moment and all I could think of was getting her home, wrapping myself in her and never letting her go. Thoughts of protecting her lingered in the back of my mind, but undressing her moved to the front.

"Would you mind if we went home now?"

Lucy nodded in agreement.

Even though Lucy didn't live with me at the apartment, she was there so much that I was beginning to think of it as our home. Last year, I felt like I was just camping out there. I never let it become anything more than temporary, but this year, my greatest fear was that our time together and our life at the apartment was fleeting.

We pulled through the gate at the hunt club and I looked to Lucy. Her head was flopped back on the headrest and her eyes were closed. She had lashes that went on for days. Despite the distraction, I managed to apply the brakes and let the truck roll to a stop.

"Lucy." Her name rolled off my tongue like melting butter as I unbuckled my seatbelt.

167

She didn't lift her head. Lucy just loosened the muscles in her neck and let her head roll to the side, flashing a sleepy smile at me.

The way the moonlight made the light in her eyes dance captivated me. The way her hair hung in waves caressing her face, the curve in by her eye and out along her cheek, I envied being able to touch her face all the time like that. The way her breasts heaved when she breathed made me thankful that she'd left those top two buttons undone from earlier. She wasn't just beautiful, she was smart, the smartest, and I was constantly wondering what she was thinking. Did she love me as much as I loved her? I loved her so much the answer to that question would never matter.

At the end of the smile, she ran her tongue slowly over her lower lip. It peeped out for just a moment, just long enough to entice me, before she bit her lip. That little act, so subtle, so innocent, so sexy, it caused my pulse to quicken. I had to shift in my seat, in my pants, to allow for my growing erection. I wouldn't cheapen Lucy by taking her right there in the Bronco, but I'd sure like to get things started.

I leaned over her, brushing my nose against her and locking our eyes as I found the lock for her seatbelt. She cupped my face in her hands, tilting my head back and granting access to my Adam's apple. That seemed to be a go to spot for Lucy and it worked. Adam's apple equaled erogenous zone and I'd never known it until Lucy took interest in it. She licked it and my toes lost grip in my shoes almost curling inside them. Then she applied just the right amount of suction. I tightened my grip in the seat on each side of her hips, clawing into the leather. As it turned out, I wasn't the one starting something in the truck. Seductive, that's what she was, and she didn't even know it.

"Right here," Lucy breathed into me. Since she wasn't the one steadying herself above me, her hands were free to start on my belt buckle.

"No." I moved back. I had fantasies about trying new places with her and new positions, but quick car sex was out of the question.

"Yes." She was half way in my pants.

"No. No. No." I wagged my nose across hers with each word, giving her Eskimo kisses, and arched my back, pulling away from her temptation.

Her lips barely grazed mine when she whispered, "You're no fun."

Holding my balance over her with my right hand, I found the handle to the door on her side of the truck, gave it a jerk and opened the door. I jumped out and grabbed her up in a fireman's carry.

Lucy grabbed her breath and gave a giggling squeal, "Edward, oh my God!"

I ran with her over my shoulder. All the way up the steps I went, taking them two at a time. Carrying Lucy was less taxing than carrying a bag of horse feed. It took me little to no effort at all.

The lock on the door to the apartment barely slowed me down. Once inside, I gave the door my heel and shoved it closed. I whirled Lucy around and pinned her against the back of the door. Her legs went instinctively around my waist. Behind my back, she kicked off her shoes. One flew clear across the living room, making a crashing thud when it landed, and the other hit the floor right behind me. I ripped my shirt over my head with one hand and held Lucy tight with the other.

Lucy started to unbutton her shirt further.

"No. No," I told her. "That's my job."

She giggled, excited with anticipation. This was the most playful we'd been leading up to sex. All of the other times, it had been devouring one another prior to making love. Not that I couldn't devour her now, I tried to give it a new feel. I wanted to experience every adventure with her possible and I liked that she seemed to be enjoying it. I wanted her to enjoy me as much as I enjoyed her.

A few deep kisses and I didn't know how much more foreplay we could stand. I sat her feet to the floor and made quick handiwork with her shorts leaving her in her panties, the white button up shirt and her bra. As soon as she was free of the shorts, I pulled her back up and braced her against the door again. I did all of this while blazing a trail of kisses in spot the left bare by the undone buttons. I nudged the shirt open more to one side and ran my tongue just inside the top lace of her bra. Chill bumps sprang up on her skin and her heart was racing. I could feel her rapid breaths whisp over my neck.

The shirt she was wearing looked kind of like a man's white dress shirt and she had the sleeves rolled up and cuffed at the elbows. I knew it might be a task for her, but I asked anyway. "Can you slip your bra off and out from under your shirt?"

There was nothing sexier than a woman in nothing but a man's dress shirt. Correction, sexier would have been her wearing my white dress shirt and nothing else.

170

"I thought you said taking off my clothes was your job."

"I can't do everything here." I acted put out but leaned her away from the door enough to snap the hook in the back.

Lucy let out a little bit of a yelp followed by a series of laughs as she shimmied out of the contraption.

"God, I love your laugh!"

"And, I love everything about you." Lucy's chest heaved and she arched, bucking her hips into me.

I loved the white shirt too. I cupped one of her breasts through the shirt. This was too much. I had to have her. With one hand I got my jeans and boxers down just enough to free myself. I slipped her panties to the side. From the moisture in them, I could tell she was as ready as I was, but I made the offer anyway. "If this isn't comfortable, tell me."

She ground against my hand, slipping my thumb inside. "Edward, please."

I held her still and took her, right there against the door. A sheen of sweat broke out over both of us. The lace of the panties was harsh and scraped against me. It broke my concentration and I finally couldn't take the scratching anymore. They were little more than strings so I gave them a snatch and they snapped like a broken rubber band.

"Edward!" Lucy screamed and I could feel her tense around me.

In the times we'd been together, she'd never screamed my name before. No one had ever screamed my name before. It was exhilarating.

I drilled into her. "Say my name again." I growled in a voice that I didn't recognize as my own.

Lucy dug her nails into my back and let out another scream when I hit a spot inside her again. "Edward!"

I pressed close to her grinding everything I had against her as I thrust once more. "Lucy, are you almost there?" I knew the answer, but I wanted to hear her say it.

"Oh God, yes, Edward!"

"Tell me when."

Three more passes in and up her and she cried out, "Now, Edward, yes, now!"

As she was rattling through hers, shaking around me, against me, I found mine. I was still amazed by the feeling. It was inconceivable to me that I'd ever had sex with anyone else because with her it was so different, so much more than I'd ever experienced and so much more than I'd ever imagined it could be.

"Lucy..." I bared into her and we clung to one another. I reached for her hands and clinched them in mine. My head rested on the door and buried in her hair. I was drenched with sweat, hers, mine, ours.

My breathing wasn't even back to normal when Lucy prodded me, "I love it when you do that to me. Do you like it too?"

"Lucy, how could you even ask? There's nothing in the world I enjoy more. Nothing."

I carried Lucy to the shower and while there, we christened it. After we showered, I led her to the kitchen and made us a snack of crackers and cheese. We christened the kitchen counter too. Eventually we then passed out together on the couch. Somewhere around 2:00 a.m. I carried Lucy to bed. From the couch to the bed, she never batted an eye to wake. I crawled beneath the covers and watched her through the darkness. Just having Lucy in my bed was a novelty to me. I knew I risked wishing our lives away, but I laid there wishing that the next few years would pass in a flash so I could skip to the part where she fell asleep in my arms every night and I awoke to her next to me every morning. I wanted this as much as I'd ever wanted to be a doctor and I'd wanted that for as long as I could remember.

The phone rang early the next morning. The light hadn't even started to peek around my make shift curtains. By the second ring both Lucy and I were startled awake.

I'd left the cordless on the bedside table. Waving my hand over the top, it took three passes before I found it and the third ring got out.

"Hello?" groggily, I answered.

"Hey. It's Maggie. I'm on my way to get Lucy. Make sure she's up. I'll be there in ten minutes." Maggie sounded frantic.

"What's wrong?" I asked her and Lucy rubbed the sleep out of her eyes as she did her best to pay attention to the part of the conversation that she could hear.

"I'll tell you when I get there. I'm on my way," she repeated herself.

Maggie was gone and the line was vacant before I could question her further.

Lucy heard half of the conversation and was already searching the floor for her clothes by the time I hung up.

173

"I'm sure Maggie's bringing you clothes."

"Yeah, but I can't be naked when she shows up." Lucy pulled her shirt over her head while I enjoyed the view until the last possible second.

Putting my feet to the floor I grumbled, "This isn't quite what I had in mind when I pictured waking up next to you."

"What? Scrambling about worried that my parents have found out about us and are going to kill us isn't your idea of fun?"

Although she joked about it, I could tell she was frightened. I thought about when my dad caught B with a boy and what followed. Lucy wasn't the only one a little scared after those thoughts.

"Oh, shit!" I started to scramble for my clothes too. "Mr. Watson's going to kill us both!"

"It's not him I'm worried about." Lucy pushed the bathroom door closed. From inside I could hear her clearly. "It's my hormonal mother that I'm worried about."

It was ten minutes on the mark when the pounding started up the stairs. The heavy footsteps got louder the farther up they came. They were so loud that I feared they weren't Maggie's little feminine feet that were making them. The muscles in my chest tightened. I was dressed and so was Lucy, but she was still in the bathroom so I'd have the face the music alone if it was her father.

The pounding on the door started next. It was more ferocious than the footsteps. My heart raced, the same pace probably as when I held Lucy through her orgasm last night, but completely different. My palms were as clammy, but it wasn't the same at all. One look at me and Mr. Watson

174

would know what had gone on with us. He'd know instinctively why she was here and what we'd done. I didn't regret it. That's not why my heart raced or my palms were sweating. No, I feared he would take her away.

The door to the apartment shook with every knock it took and the word knock, knocking, was so mild of a description of the beating the door was taking. I stood there almost frozen with my hand on the knob, working up the courage to turn it, as the reverberations from the pounding came through it and rang through the bones in my hand and my arm.

"Oh, come on!" Maggie screamed and gave the door a swift kick. Relieved to hear her, I snatched open the door to see her still drawing back her foot.

Maggie was completely winded from taking the steps at such a pace and giving the door the beating of its life. Like me, the door was having a similarly opposite experience this morning than it did last night.

Lucy stepped into the living room, fresh faced and confident that Maggie had come to warn us of the pending implosion of our romance. Winded, gasping for air from running up the stairs, and fuzzy headed from being fresh out of her bed as well, Maggie relieved us of our fears. Unfortunately, she leveled other news square at Lucy's heart.

"Wilson... Knox... is dead," Maggie huffed and puffed.

"What??!!!" Lucy shrieked. Her eyes fixed on Maggie.

I covered my mouth and watched as Lucy's eyes began to pool. Seeing Maggie rush to take her hands, I stayed back.

Maggie settled her breathing and spoke calmly. "Lucy, we've got to go. I've got to get you home. I told your dad you were in the bathroom when he called my house this morning. He wanted you to come straight home and I told him I'd drive you so we have to go. Maggie handed Lucy the clothes she'd brought with her. "Put these on and hurry."

Lucy was dazed. She held out her hands, but the clothes were like water running through them and falling to the floor. Tears slipped down her cheeks, but there were no words. I recognized that look from the mirror image of myself in the days after we lost Anne.

Maggie threw her arms around Lucy and held her. I moved around them and picked up the shirt, then the pants, underwear, socks, all the things that represented a living person. I wiped my own eyes. Two people I knew were now dead. I didn't know him well, but I knew he was too young to be dead. Anne was too young too. Lucy, she was young. From my knees, with her clothes in my hand, I looked up at her. The awe, the love, I felt for her, the thought of something happening to her. It would surely kill me.

Chapter 16

Thursday, July 3, 1997. Time stopped for Lucy that day.

I wrapped my arms around Lucy. "I'm so sorry about Will." I kissed her on her forehead and for once I felt no resentment toward him when it came to Lucy's affections.

The first thing I found out when I came back to Thomson last month was that Lucy was dating Wilson Knox. Instinctively, I hated him. He had what was mine and I wanted her back. In the moments I witnessed them together I could have killed him, but as soon as Lucy broke up with him, told me that dating him was a charade, I felt nothing toward him. Now, finding out that he was dead and without even knowing the details surrounding his death, I could only feel sorry for him.

Lucy didn't say anything and Maggie led her away. Before Maggie closed the door behind them, she instructed me, "Get dressed and come to the Watson's in thirty minutes. I'll tell them I called you. Lucy's going to need us."

I nodded, "I'll be there."

Dawn was breaking and as soon as I turned onto Lee Street toward the Watson home, I could see a police car parked out in front. That was peculiar.

I pulled along the curb and parked behind the cop car. I got out and rushed to the house. Up the steps I ran on to the porch. I avoided the doorbell, remembering that it played "Dixie" loud enough to wake the neighbors three streets over. I gave the door three swift pops with my knuckles instead.

"Oh, thank God you're here," Maggie answered the door with Lily behind her.

The two girls came out onto the porch. They circled me.

"You're going to have to tell where Lucy really was last night." Lily said, keeping her voice low. Apparently she already knew Maggie covered for us.

"What? Why?" I didn't understand.

Maggie followed with an answer. "They're on their way to talk to my parents and my parents won't lie. You're going to have to go in there and throw yourself on the sword."

"Why would they have to lie? What's going on?" I demanded. "Are you implying the police are on the way to talk to your parents? Why?"

Lily grabbed me by the arms and calmly stated. "Wilson Knox was murdered."

"And a wad of Lucy's hair was found in his hand," Maggie added.

"Excuse me?!!!" I took two steps back and pulled away from Lily's grasp. "You mean to tell me the police think Lucy had something to do with him...his..." I couldn't bring myself to say the word, to finish the question. The idea that Lucy could hurt him was so farfetched that I couldn't imagine how anyone would think that.

"You're going to have to tell them," Lily insisted.

"You're her alibi," Maggie added, seething with frustration.

There were no words to describe the shock I was in. The color drained from my face and I knew

178

my days with Lucy were numbered. There's no way her parents would let us continue as things had been once I confessed that we were spending the night together.

Maggie held the door open and Lily prodded me to go inside. In the living room I saw Mr. Watson and Mrs. Watson sitting on the couch with Lucy between them. Mr. Watson appeared to have thrown on the first thing he found which amounted to a wrinkled mess. Mrs. Watson was still in her nightgown and robe.

The same sheriff's deputy, the older heavy-set one that had come out when Lucy went missing last year, was there and just like then he was doing all of the talking. He was dressed as a deputy should be, but looked haggard the way one might who had been up all night.

"You don't have to answer anything, Lucy," I first heard Mr. Watson advise her. I was immediately struck with the confusion of whether he was acting as her father or her lawyer.

"I think she needs to tell me how her hair came to be found in the victim's hand. I really want an answer to this."

"You don't even know it's her hair!" Mr. Watson rose from the couch and challenged the deputy. "You just found the body and there's no way you've had any sort of testing done on it."

"He has a name," Lucy cried. "He's not the body! He's Will! Wilson Knox!"

"Be quiet Lucy!" Rubbing her belly, a very pregnant Mrs. Watson ordered her.

"How do I know it was hers? She had a very public fight with him at her own birthday party and there were at least a dozen people that saw. My own daughter was one of them."

"And what does that prove?" Mr. Watson barked back. "Teenagers fight, in public. It's what they do."

"Well, I'm just saying, the hair was there and if it walks like a duck and quacks like a duck..."

"Wow, Harold! Is that your thirty years of investigative experience talking?" Mr. Watson then mimicked the deputy by repeating the duck correlation.

"Excuse me," I finally caught a chance to interrupt them and make my presence known.

"Now's not a good time, son," deputy told me.

"I just thought I would ask if you have any idea when the..." again I couldn't say the word.

Maggie took over and she was not as tongue tied as I was, "When was he killed?"

Lucy shrieked as if she was hearing the word for the first time.

"We're guessing the time of death was around midnight," the deputy replied. "Neighbors on the street heard what they thought were gun shots and one by one started calling us."

"Guessing?" Mr. Watson rolled his eyes. "There you go with that stellar detective work again, Harold. I'm going to recommend you for a raise when this is all over with."

Deputy Harold gritted his teeth like a rabid pit-bull and held back growling at Mr. Watson. "I've half a mind to arrest you for obstruction."

"I'd like to see you try!" I'd never heard Mr. Watson so sarcastic before.

Lily poked me. "Now! Tell them now!"

"Tell me again why you think Lucy had anything to do with this." I stepped out of Lily's reach and further into the thick of things. All the while, Lucy watched me through tear filled eyes. If I could have snapped my fingers or twitched my nose and made all of this go away for her, I would have.

Deputy Harold rattled off his list of suspicions and topped it off with, "I know she wasn't at the McCorkle girl's house last night."

"How do you know that?" Mr. Watson again jumped to Lucy's defense.

"Because I called there after I called you looking for her this morning when you told me she was there."

Mr. Watson turned to Lucy and she dropped her head. Naturally she would be ashamed to admit to her father where she'd been, let alone what she'd been doing. I didn't fault her for that.

Deputy Harold continued, "Mrs. McCorkle answered the phone and told me she hadn't seen your daughter except when she dropped off her car the night before."

"She wasn't at the McCorkle's because she was with me." I did it.

I felt the pat on my back and the whispered thank you's from Maggie and Lily, but Mr. Watson shot daggers at me. Mrs. Watson dropped Lucy's hand and inched away from her.

The deputy looked completely befuddled as I went on. "We had dinner at Kent's around 8:30 p.m. I still have the receipt at my place and I can get that for you. After Kent's we drove home and turned in for the night."

Mr. Watson covered his face and flopped back down on the couch.

"Then how did he end up with a hand full of her hair in his fist and his face all scratched up like he'd been in a fight with a cat?" The deputy was losing his patience as he started to realize he had no case to make against Lucy.

"I don't know. I just know Lucy Meeks was with me from sometime in the afternoon after she got off work at the kennel at the Wrightsboro Hunt Club until about thirty minutes ago. Plus, I think it's already established that you don't know that it is her hair."

"Now you listen here boy we don't take kindly to smart asses in these parts!"

"But you take kindly to dumb asses?" I could not help myself. Only a real dumb ass would continue after Lucy with so little to go on as he had.

"I've half a mind..." The deputy was promptly cut off by Lily.

"Deputy Harold, I think if you had a chance to rest and regroup, you would be able to use your full mind and understand that my sister had nothing to do with this. Now, if you don't mind, our entire family has had quite the shock this morning with learning of the death of our dear family friend." Lily took me by the arm and moved the two of us out from in front of the door leading back into the foyer, clearing a path for the deputy to leave.

Deputy swatted his hat against his britches and looked back at Mr. Watson, "She did lie about her whereabouts, you know."

Mr. Watson shirked his disappointment in Lucy that sprang up on his face after learning where she'd spent the night and defended her once more. "Well, if teenagers sneaking around behind their parents' backs was a crime, you'd have to clear out the jail of all the armed robbers, rapists and murderers to make room for them. In fact, I dare say there'd be a cell with your daughter's name on it too so I'd watch casting stones if I were you."

Mrs. Watson stood from the couch. "Harold Watts, you should be ashamed of yourself. I've known you my entire life and I've considered you a good law man until now. I've seen some questionable cases come through the office and I never said anything because it wasn't my place. We defended people you arrested and sometimes I suspected that their version of events were true, but I felt you had your reasons, good reasons. Today, I'm questioning you. I want to know when you decided to care more about the notches in your belt numbering your arrests and less about the truth? What happened to you?"

"This isn't about me." He snapped back. "This is about finding who killed the Knox boy."

"And I hope you mean that." Lucy finally stood up and, when she did, she took her mother's hand. "If you don't mind, my sister is right, we've had quite a shock this morning and we don't want to keep you from finding the person who did this to Wilson."

The whole lot of us was on our feet and looking at Deputy Harold, waiting for him to accept his defeat and leave. None of us uttered another word.

As soon as the deputy left, Mr. Watson asked the girls to take Mrs. Watson back upstairs. Maggie and Lily did as he asked. Lucy started to go with them, but he caught her by the arm. "Not you, Lucy. I need to have a word with you and Edward."

As soon as Mr. Watson stopped Lucy from helping with her mother, she came back to me. I took her in my arms and stroked her head. "Lucy, I'm so sorry about Wilson."

Mr. Watson followed the girls into the hall. He stopped at the bottom of the staircase and watched as they started up with his wife. I watched him as I held onto Lucy.

"I know." Lucy clutched around me. Both of her arms were tight to my torso and she pressed her head to my chest. "What are we going to do? I can't lose you over this."

"You won't ever lose me. I promise." I kissed the top of her head.

Mr. Watson stepped back into the room. Keeping Lucy in my hold and taking small steps, I inched us back.

Mr. Watson didn't start in on us right away. The most I could hear from him was hard, ragged breaths, and that was from across the room. He was mad, but he was trying to control his anger.

I loosened my grip on her and Lucy turned to face Mr. Watson. "I'm so sorry, Daddy."

"No 'Boyd' today Lucy? I mean, that's what you've called me all this time so why start with Daddy today?" He all but accused her of trying to manipulate him.

"I don't know," she replied.

"Cop out!" He barked. "Why today, Lucy?"

"Because of all days I need my father, it's today! I just found out one of my best friends was murdered for Christ's sake!"

"So last night, when you told your mother and I that you were going to Maggie's you were an adult, making adult decisions and doing adult things, but today you want to be a child again? Am I getting this right?"

"That's not what I said!"

Mr. Watson spun around, ran his hands through his thinning hair, scratched the back of his head feverishly and shouted at Lucy like I wasn't even standing there. "You understand this could be you tied to a fence and gutted? Do you understand?!! We wouldn't have known where to find you or..." He huffed and rubbed at his face to satisfy his frustration.

I flinched as much as Lucy did. I wasn't sure if Mr. Watson described Wilson like that for the shock value of getting his point across to Lucy or if that was what had actually happened to poor Wilson. Either way, the mental image painted by Mr. Watson caused my stomach to churn and left Lucy shaking with revolt. I also doubted he'd ever yelled at her before. He was always so mild mannered and even tempered especially when it came to dealing with his daughters.

"And you," he turned to me. "I trusted you!"

"Yes, sir. I'm sorry, sir."

He lowered his voice, but we still felt his fury. "Sorry for what? I told you she couldn't take another heart break so this was your answer?"

"No sir, it's just..." I started, but Lucy finished.

185

"We love each other." She clutched my hand in an attempt to show solidarity.

"You love each other?" He shook his head. "You are only seventeen! What do you know about love?"

That really fired Lucy up. I felt her indignation through the strength in her hand as she gripped mine with a force that rubbed my bones together. "I know just as much about love as you and my mother did at your age! The only difference is I won't take twenty years to make good on it."

"Mr. Watson, please don't be mad with Lucy. If anyone's to blame, it's me. I'm older and..."

"Now's not the time to be the hero. I blame both of you. If there's one thing I can't stand, that's a liar and right now the both of you are liars and I think you need to get out of my sight until I decide what to do about you. Lucy, say your goodbyes to Edward and Maggie and get to your room. And, you better not go to your mother about this. She's got enough on her right now. Do I make myself clear?"

Lucy didn't budge. "What about Edward? You can't do to me what your mother did to you."

"This isn't about me or my mother, Lucy. This is about you lying."

I watched with wonder. He might have been furious with Lucy, but he never threatened her as my father would have threatened me or beat me if he was as mad with me as Mr. Watson was with Lucy. It wouldn't have mattered who was standing around to witness either. Nothing would have kept him from raising a hand to me.

"Go Lucy," I urged her. "I'll call you later."

Lucy looked to me and nodded. "Promise?"

"Of course I promise."

Lucy smiled at me and then shot a scowl at her father. "You won't keep us apart." It was reluctantly, but Lucy released my hand and left to find Maggie.

I figured it was as good a time as any to leave, but Mr. Watson stopped me. He'd just ordered me to leave moments before but now he ordered me to stay.

"Not so fast." He flopped back into his chair, that recliner I'd seen him sit in so many times when he watched the Braves on TV. "Take a seat."

"Yes, sir."

I did like he asked. I took a seat on the couch, across the room from him. I didn't know what he was going to say to me. I feared the worst. He was going to tell me to stop seeing Lucy. I just knew it.

"I told you I love you like a son and I meant that. I know I agreed for you to date Lucy, but I'll admit I don't know what to do with the two of you right now." Mr. Watson leaned over propping his head in his hands atop his elbows that were resting on his knees. "I can't have her lying and sneaking around. One day you'll be a father and you'll understand."

I didn't know what to say other than repeat, "Yes, sir."

Mr. Watson was curious with his next question. "Have you decided what you're doing yet?"

"Doing?" I didn't know what he was talking about.

"Have you even considered joining the Navy like I recommended?"

"I was hoping to hear back from the college before I had to think about that."

"Oh," he hung his head and paused.

He started again and he was more direct. "You love her, but you're not thinking about your future, a future with her. You're only thinking about getting through one day to the next. I want you to think about what kind of life you will have with her when you are struggling to pay back student loans the size of two house payments? I mean, that's what you'll have if you succeed with your current plan."

We sat in silence for a minute or two. I really didn't know what to say. I think he read my mind.

"I know you don't want to be away from her, but let's face it. She's got another year of high school and the odds of you getting accepted into college in August after applying this late is slim and none. I'm going to make this real simple for you, don't call Lucy and don't try to see her until you have at least spoken to the recruiter. You need to get your priorities straight."

I wouldn't break my promise to Lucy. I had to call her, but I wouldn't defy her father again. I went straight from the Watson house to the recruiter's office in Augusta. I waited in the parking lot for them to open. While I waited I wondered what really happened to Wilson Knox. The morning had started off with the shocking news of his death and somewhere along the way it got derailed from that event. I felt guilty for that. He was a person and he deserved to be more than an afterthought in mine and Lucy's lives.

Chapter 17

I plucked out my phone from my pocket, the same cell phone I had purchased the day before I lost Anne. I rarely used it, but I carried it everywhere. I dialed the number to Lucy's house. It rang three times and Mr. Watson answered. It was Thursday around 11:00 a.m., Mr. Watson shouldn't have been home, but he was. He'd likely stayed there to deal with the aftermath of news of Wilson Knox.

"Mr. Watson, I spoke with the recruiter," I told him.

He tempered his words. I could tell he couldn't believe I'd already done it. "How did it go?"

"Fine."

"Have you made a decision?"

I was offended at his question. "Of course not. I won't do anything of the kind without talking to Lucy about it first."

"She's seventeen and you're talking about consulting with her as if she were your..." He held his tongue and didn't finish the sentence.

I believe the word he kept to himself was "wife." I hoped she would be one day, but, for now, I understood where he was coming from. I hoped he would understand the same about me. I knew his history with Lucy's mother and, of all people, he should be sympathetic to what we were going through.

"You know I love her sir, so of course I would talk to her about this. I will always do her the courtesy of taking into account her feelings on things that will impact her. Always."

"What does your gut tell you to do?"

"It tells me to talk to her and consider her opinion."

"No, what does your gut tell you to do, join the Navy and salvage your financial future or go in debt up to your eyeballs to pay for college?"

"With all due respect, you told me that you wouldn't let me speak to Lucy again until I talked to the recruiter. I did like you told me and now I need to talk to Lucy about this."

I could almost see him shaking his head with frustration through the phone.

"Mr. Watson, I know our actions have disappointed you. Please tell me what we can do to move past this?"

"I don't know, son. I just don't know."

"May I please come by the house tonight? I'll be fine just to sit on the front porch with her. I promise, we won't lie or sneak around anymore."

"I understand that forbidding the two of you to see one another would just drive her to you more. I don't think you're a bad kid. In five or ten years, I'd pick you for her. I'd pick you now, but I want you to slow it down. Your future, her future, your future together depends on it. The both of you need to stop rushing everything. I realize what's happened to you. You lost your sister so you're in this mode of living every day to its fullest. I understand. I do. I know Lucy's about to go into the same mode thanks to her friend's death. I was once your age and as Lucy so aptly pointed out this morning, I made some mistakes. It took me a long time to learn from those mistakes. One of the things I learned is love's like a fire. It can burn fast and burn itself out or it can burn slow and go on forever. You have to stoke it, but not rush it and smother it. You have all your lives to watch it burn. Do you understand?"

"I think so, sir."

"Come by the house tonight," he finally relented.

"Thank you! Thank you, sir, thank you so much!" It was hard to keep my excitement and gratitude contained.

I hung up with Mr. Watson and continued through Harlem toward Dearing and Thomson. The light on my phone indicating I had messages waiting blinked. Before putting the phone away I checked the messages. The two ladies scheduled to have riding lessons that afternoon phoned me to cancel. One needed to use the afternoon to make food to take over to the Knox family. The other cancelled because she was afraid to leave the house with a murderer on the loose.

The cancellations freed up my entire afternoon and I was glad for it. Wilson Knox had not been far from my mind all morning. I wondered what had really happened to him, how he died and why. If there was one thing that was certain right now it was that this day should be about him, but somehow it had turned into being about me and Lucy. I felt guilty and like we'd been terribly selfish. The more I was left alone with my thoughts the more of a sense of loss set in. I didn't really know it, but I was starting to grieve for him.

Needing to know what happened, what the word around town was, I decided to go to the one place in Thomson, short of a beauty parlor, that would have information. I went straight to Neal's Bar-B-Que. Neal's was the place to be for men folk on Thursdays and Fridays at lunch.

True to form the parking lot was packed. I recognized more than one car in the lot as I pulled the Bronco into a spot.

Also true to form, the dining area was packed with men. I counted three women in the whole place. One was in the kitchen, another was behind the register and the last of the three was in line in front of me with a list of to-go orders spanning an entire sheet of paper with Huber's letterhead on top.

Huber was the largest of the chalk companies. It was hard to miss it on both sides of the road between Thomson and Wrens. I only knew as much as I did about it because Whitney Knox invited me to go swimming with her and her friends at the family pond right after I arrived in town last summer. I didn't find out soon enough that her idea of swimming was skinny dipping and her idea of the pond was the chalk mine on the property that her family had leased to Huber and, conveniently, none of her friends showed up that afternoon. As much as Whitney was not my type of girl, I never wished her ill, I felt sorry for her last year when Lucy caused her to get thrown from her horse. Today, I felt even worse for her. I wondered how she was taking her brother's death.

The woman from Huber went on and on listing off one order after another. My thoughts floated between Whitney Knox and wishing that the woman would hurry up and finish. I hadn't had breakfast that morning and it was a little after noon. My stomach was growling and I was hungry.

I glanced around the room to see the faces that went with the vehicles in the parking lot. I spotted Mr. Westmorland, another of the members from the hunt club. He waved at me and pointed to the empty seat across from him. Seating was sparse so I mouthed the words "Thank you" to him for saving me a spot.

The whole restaurant was buzzing with speculation over Wilson Knox. I heard his name in hushed conversations from one corner of the dining room to the other. It seemed everybody in there had heard some snippet of what had happened but from my place in line I couldn't' get a full perspective from any of them.

Nearly twenty minutes after I first walked in I finally had my plate. Chopped pork, hash, potato salad and a couple of slices of white bread, this was the best Bar-B-Que around shy of Sconyers in Augusta. It smelled divine and looked like enough for me to have for lunch and dinner.

I found the chair Mr. Westmorland saved for me and took a seat. A couple of introductions and swigs of my sweet tea later and I had my courage to ask what they'd heard about Wilson. I found the men at the table could rival any woman with their enthusiasm for gossip. While I played ignorant and took bites of my lunch, Mr. Westmorland and his friends were more than happy to fill me in.

"Whoever did it wanted him to be found," the salt and pepper haired man in the chair to Mr. Westmorland's right observed. Mr. Pope was his name.

I shoved the mouthful of chopped pork to the inside of my cheek and asked, "Why do you say that?"

Mr. Pope followed up, "What was left of him was strung up to the stop sign at the end of Dixie Drive. It's not like they went to the trouble to hide the body. It was right out in the middle of a neighborhood and fifty people were gawking over him by the time the police arrived."

The street name rang a bell, but I couldn't think of why as they gentleman continued adding pieces of the conversation.

Mr. Westmorland wiped his mouth with his napkin. "I just can't believe such a thing would happen here in Thomson. Augusta, yes, murders happen all the time there. Gruesome stuff like this, but not here, not in Thomson."

"I feel sorry for his parents. They've had a time with that boy." Mr. Donaldson was another of Mr. Westmorland's friends and he sat to my left. He seemed to know the Knox family very well. "The boy got kicked out of the private school a while back and they had to enroll him in Thomson High."

I chewed and listened. The tone of Mr. Donaldson's voice told me he knew the whole story about Wilson getting expelled from school. The upturn in the side of his nose told me he didn't think highly of the public school. He clearly ran in circles where the kids were above a public school education.

Mr. Westmorland was quick to point out that Wilson seemed to be doing better at the public school, thriving even. "From what I heard he went to prom with Boyd Watson's step-daughter, the one that works at the kennel."

"And his parents worried about him being gay?" Mr. Donaldson snickered. "I can't imagine any man being able to keep his hands off of that one."

Mr. Donaldson was getting under my skin with his comments about Lucy and his superior attitude. I clinched my fork and refrained from stabbing him with it. Thomson didn't need two murders in one day.

"Didn't Boyd's wife used to own a house on Dixie Drive?" Mr. Pope asked and that's when I realized why the name of the street was familiar.

Suddenly bells and whistles started going off in my head. Wilson was a friend of Lucy's. He was found tied to a stop sign on the street where she grew up and Deputy Harold believed he had a wad of Lucy's hair in his hand. My mind was circling back to some of the first words in the conversation as the men continued without my full attention. "Someone wanted him found," is what was said.

Over my own thoughts I heard one of the men say the word "firecracker" and I snapped back to reality. "Excuse me? What was that about firecrackers?"

Mr. Westmorland repeated what his friend had just said, "I heard that the remnants of firecrackers were found on the ground around the body."

The gentleman to my left continued, "I ran into Harold Goodson this morning and y'all know how he is. He's not supposed to talk about cases, but more often than not he can't help himself."

All three men chuckled. Apparently they were talking about Deputy Harold, but nothing about this was a laughing matter to me.

Mr. Donaldson went on, "Harold said it appeared roman candles were shot directly into his torso from close range. The boy's insides were blown out of his back."

I hadn't finished eating, but I was done. If I kept picturing that image, it would be a new weight loss plan. I might not ever be able to eat again.

My parents never gave me full disclosure regarding how Anne died. They never told me exactly what happened to her, but I did hear them mention firecrackers in their discussions of her each time I overheard them. Anne and firecrackers. Wilson and firecrackers. Strange.

I wasn't normally inconsiderate and I never left anyone to clean up behind me, but today I did. I left my tray on the table and headed for the door of Neal's. I yelled the obvious back to Mr. Westmorland and his friends, "I've got to go!"

If there hadn't been so many people in the restaurant I'd have ran for the door. Instead, I had to weave and dodge and shove past other diners. "Excuse me," I said so many times until I shouted at the final patron standing between me and the exit. I had to get to Lucy as fast as I could.

As crazy as it was to think it, I couldn't stop. It scared the Hell out of me, but I feared it was true. There was a connection between Anne's death and Wilson Knox's.

I sprinted across the parking lot, flung open the door and slid into the driver's seat. I slammed the key in, turned the ignition and floored the gas in one fluid moment. I peeled out onto the highway slinging all of the crush and run that was beneath my tires over the cars and parking lot behind me. The back end of the truck fishtailed right before hitting the pavement. My cell phone was in the passenger's seat where I'd left it and it slid from one side to the other, catching my attention. I reached for it and dialed my mother.

I hardly allowed her to answer with her heavy accented, "Hello."

"Mama, it's me. Something horrible has happened," I started to explain.

"Are you alright?" I'm sure the urgency I conveyed frightened her.

"Yes, ma'am..."

"And Lucy?"

"Yes, but Mama, I need you to tell me exactly what happened to Anne."

"Oh, no, Edward. You don't ever need to worry yourself with that. No, no, son."

"Mama, please. The unthinkable has happened here in Thomson and I think maybe..." I cleared my throat, afraid to make my mother relive the details of my sister's death. I didn't want to do that to her, but I needed to know. I feared this might all be connected and not just one murder to the next, but to me and maybe to Lucy. "Mama, tell me about the firecrackers."

Through the crackle of the bad connection and the wind noise from the poor seal of the old hard top of the Bronco, I could hear my mother burst into tears. A howl, cry like none I'd heard from her since the day the call came that Anne had been found, rang through the line.

"Mama, I'm so sorry, but I need you to tell me."

The words quaked out of her in a whisper, "They said he put a firecracker in her mouth and lit it. There was nothing left of my baby's sweet face. Her beautiful hair. I remember her dimples. Oh, God, Edward."

Absentmindedly, I'd made my way to the intersection at Hill Street and Broad. I didn't remember stopping for the light, but I had. I'd stopped far too long. When a series of honks from an angry horn behind me finished, I came to and found my face covered in tears. I'd lost my senses in the image my mother portrayed of my sister.

"It was like she didn't even matter. She wasn't even a human being," my mother sobbed. "All I can hear is her little voice calling me and no one coming. Was she alone and scared? Those things haunt me."

"They haunt me too Mama and I think the person who did it is here."

Chapter 18

On the way to find Lucy I noticed no less than ten news crews had descended on Thomson. There were ones from Augusta, ones from Atlanta and ones from as far away as Columbia, South Carolina. It was a different town, but a very familiar scene for me. This was exactly how my little college town had been descended upon in the days following Anne's disappearance.

My senses were heightened and the news crews weren't the only thing I'd noticed. There were swarms of agencies. Marked cars, unmarked cars, crime scene vans, FBI, GBI, city police, the sheriff's department, they were everywhere and in a hurry. The sleepy Georgia town was being turned inside out. Beyond the agency cars, I noticed every driver of every vehicle I passed. I only knew a handful of people in town beyond the members of the hunt club so all of the faces I saw were suspect to me. That was a familiar scene and feeling too.

My frantic trip to the Watson house was fruitless. I didn't find Lucy at home. I found Mr. Watson and he wasn't exactly pleased with me. He'd had time to process the fact that I'd gone straight to the recruiter's office after his ultimatum.

"You'd do anything for her wouldn't you?" He quizzed me on the front steps of their home. He maintained the high ground on the top step of the porch, but even from three shoulder widths away and two steps down, I didn't see him as looming over me.

This was not the time to discuss my intentions toward Lucy, but I answered anyway. "Yes, sir, I would." I told the truth as that is exactly what I came there with the intention to do, to find her and protect her. I'd give my life for her if I had to.

Mr. Watson rubbed his forehead and gritted his teeth. "She'd follow you to the ends of the Earth, you know." He didn't seem at all pleased with his confession.

I didn't know what to say. All I knew was I didn't have time to stand around with him, but couldn't bring myself to walk off and leave him standing there either. Plus, I really hoped he would tell me where she'd gone.

"Lucy would forgo all of this," he motioned to the grand white columned house behind him, "and live in a dirt hut on the far side of BFE if you asked her. One day, when you have children of your own, you'll understand how this irritates me."

Again he paused and the air filled with silence. I felt I should say something, but I wasn't sure what. Should I thank him for not behaving as my father would have? My sister B had a less than desirable suitor once. The boy was about my age, but not nearly my size. My father had me beat the shit out of the boy and dare him to come back. That was the last time we'd hear from him and B was refocused on her studies and going to college. College was her ticket away from all of us. Thinking of B and her escape led me to my response.

"I hope I'm more than Lucy's ticket to leave home."

"I'm sure you are, but my point is that she is young and she's smart, but she thinks with her heart. She always has. A family across town just lost a son. I can't begin to know how that feels, but..."

I cleared my throat as my own frustration started to grow. "Mr. Watson, the reason I'm here right now is to find Lucy. I'm not trying to take her away, so with all due respect, your focus is all wrong today. You're right, one of her best friends has been violently murdered and I have a bad feeling that's somehow related to what happened to my sister Anne." My urgency was shining through by the time I finished my last sentence.

"Excuse me? What do you mean?"

"I mean, we need to find Lucy because two people that connect Wilson and my sister are me and Lucy. Lucy saw something or someone last night that spooked her and I need to know what or who it was."

"I don't understand. You're saying the murders are related and you think Lucy has something to do with it?"

"No, no," I shook my head. "I don't know much, but from what I've heard, firecrackers were used to kill both of them. Firecrackers, that can't be a coincidence. I'm scared."

"She's at the kennel. I'll go with you," Mr. Watson insisted. "Just let me tell Mary where I'm going."

My stomach dropped at the thought of her being at the kennel alone or anywhere alone for that matter. "No! I'll get Lucy. Please stay here and look after Mrs. Mary and Lily."

"Oh, shit, Lily! She's at my office by herself!"
Mr. Watson spun around and dug his keys out of his
pocket. He yelled back in the screen door on the
front of the house to tell Mrs. Mary he'd be right
back.

I dashed back to my truck. "I'll find her and
we'll be right back." I slammed the door, cranked the
truck and was on my way, backing out of the
driveway as quickly as I'd pulled in.

I got caught at every light, behind every slow
driver and the final stretch of road between me and
the hunt club was detoured due to a repaving project
at which point I fell in behind a funeral procession.
All that was missing to this true driving treat was
rain. Every obstacle provided more time to conjure
images of something terrible happening to Lucy. I
was out of my mind with worry.

Finally, I pulled through the gate onto the
hunt club property and was certain that my worst
fear was about to be realized. I couldn't see Lucy's
Mustang parked in the yard of the kennel. She
always parked in the same spot near a cedar tree, but
it wasn't there. I pounded my fists on the steering
wheel, frustrated and scared, and then from the
corner of my eye, I saw her car. She parked where I
normally parked at the front of the hunt barn. I had
never been more relieved to see her car. The blood
returned to my face and my stomach started to settle.

I searched the kennel to no avail. I searched
the apartment. No Lucy. I ran back down the steps
as fast as my feet would carry me and I was
screaming her name, calling for her the whole way
into the stables.

I stopped in the middle of the barn, spinning and fisting my hair in my hands. "Lucy!" The word coming with such force that it strained my throat.

At the far end of the barn Lucy stepped out of Blueberry's stall. "Edward, what is it?"

I stood frozen. I was so relieved to see her that I couldn't move. All I could do was stare at her and try to keep from losing my lunch.

Lucy looked like it was any other day of working at the kennel and she was doing what she did most days during her lunch break. Blueberry would always be Lily's horse in one regard, but she was Lucy's horse in all ways that mattered because Lucy was the one that took care of her. She was brushing down Blueberry after mucking the stall. The only difference in her today was that her face was stained with tears.

"Edward!" Lucy said with more force.

Flashes of what I imagined happened to Anne and what had now happened to Wilson Knox ran through my head. I was so relieved to have found Lucy safe. I still didn't move. I just stood there saying a prayer, thanking God that I'd found her. Lucy called my name again and I rejoined reality and noticed she was in front of me. I ran to her and scooped her up in my arms.

"You're okay. Thank God." I didn't want to ever let her go.

Lucy buried her head in my chest and cried until there were no more tears. "I just can't believe what they're saying about Wilson."

I was relieved Lucy heard the details and I wasn't the one that would have to give them to her.

"Lucy, do you want me to take you home?" I made the offer after letting her cry for some ten minutes or more. I didn't want to take her home. I didn't want to let her out of my sight, but maybe she needed her family and, under the circumstances, I could completely understand.

Leaning back, Lucy wiped her eyes. "I don't want to go home. I don't want to do anything. I don't want to be anywhere. All I want is for Wilson to be okay."

Just looking at her shattered me. Lucy's eyes were blood shot and no matter how many times she wiped them, they were still dripping with tears and pleading for some level of comprehension. "Why would someone do this to him?"

Even though I thought it was connected to Anne's disappearance and what happened to her, I didn't have the answer for Lucy's question. All I could do was hold her and be with her.

"I'm so sorry." I stroked her hair from the top to the bottom, slowly, over and over again. "You can stay here as long as you like."

My mother used to tell us that sometimes it was best to just be quiet. "She'd say if you do not have anything to contribute keep your mouth closed and listen." With my mother's words in mind, I led Lucy to the bench outside of Blueberry's stall.

"Why don't we just sit?" I took a seat and motioned for Lucy to take the spot next to me.

We sat in silence with nothing but the sounds of horses rustling in their stalls and the sounds of summer creeping through the barn. Seemingly lost in her grief, Lucy laid her head on my shoulder and I draped my arm around her. Maybe holding her and being with her was comfort enough.

Despite blaming myself and the phone call I made to Lucy the night Anne disappeared, during my darkest days it was the thought of Lucy that kept me going. I would have given anything to have seen her, to have sat next to her or to have wrapped my arms around her. I hoped now that she was the one in the depths of darkness being there for her would comfort her.

Lucy didn't budge, but I heard the soft words as she asked the question, "How could anyone think I'd do such a thing to Wilson?"

It wasn't worth rehashing what she'd done to his sister last year, so I remained quiet. Plus, what Lucy did to Whitney, although dangerous, it was more of a prank than an evil act. I gathered what had happened to Wilson was pure evil. It was the stuff of horror movies, certainly not of everyday life in Thomson.

When I didn't answer, Lucy looked at me. "I just don't understand."

"I don't understand either, but we need to go. I'm supposed to take you home and we need to get there before your parents get any more worried than they already are."

Lucy picked up the case of CD's from between her feet in the floor board. She thumbed through it until she found that nearly worn out disc. She put it in the player and it began, "Black," by Pearl Jam. For a moment I was transported back to last summer.

The air conditioner was almost always on the fritz and today was no exception. The top wasn't off like last year so that was a difference. The windows were down and the air swarmed through adding only a tinge of relief from the summer heat. Lucy stretched her arm out of the window on her side and laid her head on it.

"Lucy, are you okay?"

I laid a hand on the back of her head and rubbed my hand down the locks that fell over her back. Even in my darkest moments and now in hers I still marveled at her beauty. As sad as she was, she was amazing and, like I'd told her father, I would have done anything for her. I would have taken this pain away from her and worn it as my own if only I knew how.

She didn't lift her head, she only rolled it over so she could tilt her eyes in my direction, eyes that were again filled with tears. "Did you sign up for joining the Navy?"

"We don't have to talk about that now," I replied.

"Now's as good a time as any for you to tell me you're leaving me again." A lone tear slipped down her cheek.

"I told you before I'm not leaving you."

Lucy twisted, shirking my hand on her back and I withdrew. "But you met with the recruiter."

"I didn't see that your father left me much choice."

Lucy shrugged and turned her face away.

The problem was that the Navy recruiter made a lot of sense. He gave a similar, but more thorough pitch as her father had given. The Navy offered a way to support myself, an education and a chance to see the world. Those were all things that I didn't stand a chance of doing in my current state. I was English by birth, but I'd been raised here in the states starting from so early that I'd lost my original accent. I'd not long ago become a United States citizen and joining the Navy was also a chance to serve my country. They were all compelling notions of why I should join up and straight away.

Under other circumstances, ones where I'd been allowed to talk to a rational version of Lucy, I'd likely been able to explain to her how joining would not be leaving her at all. I could have made her see joining would be a pledge to her, something that I was doing in an effort to keep her forever. It was a short-term solution to what was now my long term problem, no money, no home, no education, no employment beyond the next two months. That was no way to build a future.

While Lucy remained silent, reminders and doubts flooded my mind. Lucy was still in high school so who were we kidding? Maybe there was no future to be had by Lucy and me. Maybe we were just one another's first loves and it would fade in time. I hoped that wasn't the case. I felt it to my bones that it wasn't the case, but I'm sure that's what most young loves thought. Glancing from the road to Lucy, I wondered if this was all fleeting. The one thing I did know is that this was not the time to convince her of the good it would do the both of us if I followed her father's advice.

When we pulled up in front of her house Lucy didn't wait for me to shut the engine off let alone come around and open the door for her. She hopped out of the truck, slammed the door behind her and started for the house.

I called after her. "Lucy!"

She kept walking without one shred of an acknowledgement to me.

"Lucy!" I caught her by the arm and she snatched away. "Are you angry with me?"

"What do you think?" Lucy let out a sigh and rolled her eyes at me.

I liked to think this was just her grief and the truth was she was just mad at the world. No, this was definitely not the time to try to convince her of anything. It was however the time to ask her what had nearly slipped my mind.

"Who did you see last night?" I asked, promptly changing the subject.

Chapter 19

Lucy's eyes were blood shot from all of the crying she'd done that day and her breath caught in her throat and evidence of a memory flashed across her face.

"Lucy," I asked again, "who did you see?"

"Dwayne Richards." She paused between his first and his last names.

That was the name of the boy who'd worked at the kennel with her for the first part of the summer. It was the name of the boy who'd nearly raped her and when she fought him off he left her deep in the woods near the hunt club. Turned around, confused and desperately shaken, she was thrown out in the wild to find her way back or die trying. The latter was surely what he'd intended.

Lucy did find her way out and Dwayne Richards was basically exiled from the McDuffie County area. The way she said his name, the pause, the struggle to get it out, the fright she'd displayed last night, those things made me realize she was still tormented by what he'd done to her.

Lucy wasn't the only one he'd terrorized. I'd never known the extent of it, but he'd done something to my sister Anne the summer before when she worked at the kennel. Anne never told a soul exactly what he'd done, not even our parents, but something had happened, something so awful that she quit the kennel and came back home mid-summer. Anne was no quitter so whatever it was, it was drastic. Ever since I learned of what he tried to do to Lucy, I suspected he hadn't just tried with Anne. I feared the worst. I feared he'd succeeded.

My mind spun at the thought of him touching Lucy or Anne. It made me physically ill. I made a mental note of how I would kill Dwayne Richards if I ran into him while Lucy headed inside. With the slamming of the screen door, I found myself alone in the yard. I put my thoughts of revenge aside and hurried along to catch up with her.

The entire family was congregated in the living room and glued to the commercial for the Channel 6 news that was playing on the television. Mr. Watson was back with Lily and I was relieved to see everyone in the room safe and sound.

The newscaster gave the teaser as to what was to come, "Ahead at 6:00 p.m., a grizzly scene in Thomson, Georgia this morning has left the small community reeling. A member of the prominent Knox family was found murdered. Stay tuned for more on Channel 6 News."

Lucy eased next to her mother who was seated on the couch. Mrs. Mary inched away from her. Mrs. Watson turned her head and rubbed her protruding belly on one end of the couch. Lily scooted her knees up to her chest. There was clearly a rift between them. That was nothing new. I suspected the latest strain on their relationship was partly because of me, because of the implications of Lucy not having slept at Maggie's house last night. Despite the history between her and Mr. Watson, Lucy's mother held her to a much higher standard than she held herself. If ever it was a time for Mrs.

Mary to put judgement aside and just be a mother to Lucy, it was now.

The commercial also mentioned some happenings in Augusta and as it ended   Lily moved to Lucy's side and took a seat on the arm of the couch.

I kept my distance at the door between the living room and the foyer. Mr. Watson joined me as the opening scenes credits for one of the afternoon soap operas began.

"Did you find out who Lucy saw last night?" Mr. Watson whispered as if in passing.

I followed him into the foyer.   "Dwayne Richards." I gritted my teeth and felt the bile rise in my throat as I said his name.

"I suspected as much," Mr. Watson shook his head. "I thought I saw him last week myself."

Mr. Watson scratched his head. "Did Lucy tell you that we've been making her go to counseling for the last few months over what he did to her?"

I covered my mouth and forced the answer through, "No, sir." There was a primal urge rising in me. I turned my back and went through the front door. Without thinking I gave the first column on the house that I came to a couple of swift jabs as one would do to a punching bag. My knuckles were bloodied, but I didn't feel a thing. I wanted to scream, but not because of any pain I'd inflicted on myself. I wanted to scream out of frustration. That S.O.B. had damaged Lucy and I hadn't even known it. All these months, I'd pushed her away while I dealt with my self-absorbed issues over Anne and I never knew what Lucy was going through.

Mr. Watson emerged from the house with a wet cloth in one hand and the cordless phone in the other. He handed me the cool cloth. "Here, wipe your hands off and stop that nonsense. The only person you're hurting is yourself."

"I wish it was that bastard's face!" I wiped the blood off and didn't even flinch.

Mr. Watson started dialing the phone. "It's probably best that we came out here anyway."

I looked at him with the unspoken question of why?

"Because we need to find out if he really is back and I don't want to worry them with that until we have the answer."

Mr. Watson held the phone to his ear and from where I was I could hear it ringing through to the other end. A few rings and someone picked up. I didn't know who and I couldn't make out what was being said from that end. I could only hear that Mr. Watson's side. The jest of the conversation was that someone named Tom was going to come by on his way home from work.

"Tom Evans lives out by the Richards. I got him a pretty good settlement in his divorce. He owes me a favor. He'll let us know if he's seen the boy around."

"Daddy," Lily stuck her head out of the door. "Do you want me to start dinner?"

"That would be great, Hun." Mr. Watson offered.

It was only a little after 3:00 p.m. and they were already talking about dinner preparations. That wasn't even the remarkable part. I'd been back for weeks and I still hadn't really wrapped my mind around the changes in Lily. She reminded me of a character on one of my mother's soap operas, the young girl played by an actress that was sent away to school and then returns in a few months aged five years and played by another actress. That's how I saw Lily. She was a completely different person this year than last.

"Should I set a place for Edward, too?" Lily smiled my way.

"Yeah, that would be fine," her father nodded.

I chimed in, "Thanks, but are you sure? I'm not certain Mrs. Mary's real keen on having me around right now."

"Leave Mary to me." Mr. Watson and I were of the same mindset. There was something bigger going on here than mine and Lucy's indiscretions.

A Huber truck smeared in kaolin pulled up in front of the house about 4:30 p.m. I sat rocking on the front porch by myself. Lucy still wasn't talking to me and I figured I just needed to give her space. I also figured she was trying to keep me at arm's length to appease her mother.

As the man came closer I could read his name tag on his uniform, "Tom." He didn't have the look of a hunt club member.

Within a couple of strides of the front steps, he asked, "Hey, is Boyd around?"

"Yes, sir. Let me get him."

Mr. Watson returned to the porch upon arrival of Mr. Evans.

"Under any other circumstances I'd ask you in, but with all that's gone on..."

Mr. Evans didn't let Mr. Watson continue. He waived him off. "Oh, no, I completely understand.   Women folk don't need to know everything."

I grew up with three women so I knew keeping things from the fairer sex was rarely a good idea, but this wasn't my call. On this, I deferred to Mr. Watson's judgement and the three of us continued with a hushed toned conversation there among the rockers and swing.

"Still, let me offer you something to drink." Mr. Watson then called for Lily and she came running. "Would you get Tom a glass sweet tea?"

"Yes, sir. Hi, Mr. Evans, good to see you." Lily then returned to the house to fetch the tea.

Mr. Watson proceeded to the point. "Have you seen any sign of the Richards boy out your way?"

Mr. Evans pondered the question before he answered. "Someone's been coming in and out late at night, but could I give a definite yes or no, I couldn't. Do I suspect it's him? Yes."

"What makes you think so?" It was on the tip of my tongue to ask the same question, but Mr. Watson beat me to it.

"No one's been around much until his father died and with his mother being home alone. Well, Dwayne was as big a mama's boy as there came so there's no way he wouldn't come back now." Mr. Evans paused and as he did I recalled my memories of Dwayne Richards. I reveled in the thought of him as a mama's boy.

"Plus, it's just a feeling," he added.

"What sort of feeling? What do you mean?" That time I asked the question and left Mr. Watson calling back his words to keep from repeating me.

"My ex-wife always said that boy gave her the creeps. It's one thing for a woman to have intuition about someone, you know, women's intuition and all." Mr. Evans clammed up when Lily returned with the glass of tea for him.

Mr. Evans was having a hard time explaining the feeling he got. I nodded in agreement. I understood exactly what he was saying as I'd explained the very same thing to Lucy about Dwayne last year and listening to her intuition.

After the exchange was made, Lily left and Mr. Evans continued. "I don't know what they call it when men get it, a sixth sense or something. I'm not sure, but whatever it is, it goes off in me whenever that boy is around. It's been going off again lately. Seriously, ever since he was a little kid he's made the hair on the back of my neck stand up."

"Did you ever witness him do anything?" Mr. Watson prodded.

"I didn't, but my oldest boy did." Mr. Evans directed his attention to me as he knew I wasn't familiar with him and would need a bit more detail.

"My oldest, Chip, is about five years younger than Dwayne, so they were five and ten at the time. Someone had thrown out a litter of puppies in front of the Richards' house. That's what some folks do. They don't want 'em and drive 'em out some country dirt road, carry 'em off and pitch the pups outside the road to fend for themselves. Nature takes care of some. Others take up around someone's house and are taken pity on. Others are shot by the land owner. It's unfortunate, but a reality of country life."

"Well, anyway, ten year old Dwayne got the idea, probably from his idiot of a father, to get rid of them. They were tiny mutts and he was chasing them all over tarnation, throwing them in an old feed sack. One of the pups ran all the way to our yard. Chip was out playing on his swing set and there came Dwayne, chasing this pup and dragging the yelping bag behind him. My boy thought he was being helpful and caught it for Dwayne. Dwayne thanked him, tossed it in the bag with the others and then set off about his business. Chip followed."

"We live out on the county line and our property backs up to the Little River and the Richards are next door. So, Dwayne, with this bag full of puppies goes trudging off down toward the river and Chip followed, curious what he was going to do with the puppies. Along the way Dwayne stopped and picked up a brick, one of the ones left out in the back yard when they built our house. He continued on with the brick in one hand and the top of the sack bunched in the other. He kept going with Chip still trailing behind him."

Mr. Watson and I went on listening intently and Mr. Evans told quite the tale. "There's a bit of a drop off down to the river and when Dwayne came to the bank, and with no regard to Chip being behind him, Dwayne threw the brick in the sack, tied the top and flung it as hard as he could. Chip screamed in horror as the bag of flew down to the middle of the river. While the bag of puppies bobbed about in the water and started to sink, Dwayne turned to go. Chip was bawling his eyes out and as Dwayne walked by he threatened my boy. 'You tell a soul about this and I'll find a sack big enough for you,' he said."

"It took my wife three days to get Chip to tell her what was wrong. What had happened that had him crying all the time and clearly terrified of going outside. When he finally told, it was all I could do to keep the woman from going next door and murdering a ten year old. I shared her sentiment, but he was a boy, a stupid, cruel boy, but a boy. Anyway, we put up a six foot tall privacy fence and never let our kids play outside alone again."

"Every single time we saw that boy or his name came up, my wife, ex-wife, I mean, would immediately say, 'I wouldn't be surprised if he kills somebody one day.' You can imagine that mailbox incident wasn't real shocking to us. We kind of thought it was poetic justice that he lost a couple of fingers doing it. To this day we can hardly get Chip to go to the lake or in a river."

Mr. Evans described a couple of other strange occurrences around his property and he suspected Dwayne was behind them, but he never caught him and there was nothing he could ever prove. "My wife loved cats. She didn't want them in the house, but she thought she could keep them outside. Every time she brought one home it disappeared. It might have been a hawk or a fox that got them, but something always told me it was Dwayne. One cat turned up on our front porch, head on one step, body on another. A hawk or fox or another animal wouldn't do that. That time that feeling went off like bells and whistles, telling me something was bad wrong around there."

"I'm guessing everything stopped and that feeling went away when he left town last year?" Mr. Watson observed.

"That it did. I'm real sorry about what happened with your daughter, but yeah, it was a relief to have that boy gone."

I explained to them that Mr. Evans wasn't the only one who got a bad feeling when he was around. I also explained to them about what went on between him and Anne. "I think he might have raped her, but I'm not sure."

"I'm sorry, but I wouldn't put it past him." Mr. Evans scratched his head and curled up his nose. He was just disgusted.

After about an hour long discussion, things started to wind down. Mr. Evans provided a wealth of information about Dwayne Richards, but admitted he hadn't had much to do with him during his teenage years.

"To tell the truth, I avoided him and the entire bunch next door. If he was anything like his daddy, he's the bad combination of mean and stupid," Mr. Evans summed up.

During Mr. Evans' stories, the smell of fried pork chops floated out from the house and permeated the porch. Finally, Lily appeared at the door again.

"Y'all can come to supper whenever you're done gossiping," she teased. "Mr. Evans, I sat a place for you as well."

Mr. Evans looked down at his work boots. They were covered in the same milky white film from the chalk mine that his truck was covered in. "No, no. Thanks for the offer, but I won't track up your house. I need to be getting home."

"Nonsense." Mr. Watson stood up and opened the door wider, also making the offer.

"You haven't lived until you've had Lily's cooking." I gave Lily a wink. "I think she's trying to put White Columns out of business."

The men folk laughed, but ultimately Mr. Evans politely declined and went on his way.

Chapter 20

The red numbers on the clock flashed to the next minute, 3:18 a.m. They were so bright in the darkness that they made my blurry, sleep filled eyes sting. The room was pitch black except for the numbers. I sat up in bed. Even though I couldn't see my hands before me, I brought them to my face and rubbed my eyes.

I was startled away, but in the initial confusion between dream and reality, I wasn't completely sure if I was alone. I felt the opposite side of the bed, checking for Lucy. It seemed the only time I slept well was when Lucy was beside me and my hand only ran across the empty sheets. I stretched and exhaled, wondering when I would get another good night's sleep. Thanks to the events of the previous day, I wondered when I would ever sleep next to her again.

I was alone and I was definitely awake, but the memory of the dream started playing in my mind.

"Edward!" Anne called for me as someone chased her.

I was running in that field again. I could see the tree line. I could see Anne running. Another flash revealed who was chasing her. This time, in this version of that same old dream, I was the one chasing her.

Just shy of the woods, the woods that I could never make it to, Anne stopped. I was within reach of her when she turned around to me. She was a vision, exactly the way I remembered her. Her eyes were a light and it made my heart break because, even in the dream, the reality of her fate was ever present in my mind. She tilted her head to the side and with a warm, knowing smile, she reached in the pocket of her jacket and handed me the folded up note.

I flicked my eyes to the point of our touch when we exchanged the note. It was only a split second that I looked down, but when I looked back to her, Anne was gone. I darted my eyes from side to side. I twisted and looked at the field behind me and back to the woods ahead. She'd vanished.

I unfolded the paper and deciphered the mismatched newspaper and magazine clippings to form words and sentences. The writing on the page was something straight out of a psychotic thriller.

"Eddie, you took something of mine and now I've taken something of yours.

D."

In all of its nightmarish glory, it was the note Agent Wasden said was in Anne's coat pocket when they found it months ago. Back then, the focus was on my father. His name was Edwin and Eddie was a natural fit for a nickname. He had more than a passing connection to a woman named Diane Reneaux from our hunt club. The FBI dug deep on my father and uncovered his affair with Ms. Reneaux. They automatically assumed the D. from the note was her until they dug even deeper into her life.

During the investigation, the FBI didn't look to hard into my life. They confirmed my phone call to Lucy, but she was so far away I supposed they dismissed any connection she might have to Anne's disappearance. No one, including me, dreamed that the note was directed at me, but Eddie was also a nickname for most men named Edward.

D. had nothing to do with my father's mistress. That was just some cosmic payback for all of the awful things he'd ever done, as if his daughter being kidnapped and murdered wasn't enough.

The initials had everything to do with Dwayne Richards. I was certain of it. I distinctly remembered him calling me Eddie as if it was an insult he was slinging my way. The moment I first met Lucy came to mind. He called me that when I defended her against the way he was treating her and how we almost came to blows that morning. I could see his face as clearly as if it was anything but dark in that room and I was anything but alone.

Knowing that Dwayne Richards had murdered my sister and likely Wilson Knox as well brought no comfort. What it brought me was rage. Rage and fury coursed through me and I beat my fists against the mattress. I wanted that bastard Dwayne Richards dead, but short of calling Agent Wasden in the morning there was little I felt I could do.

The hours 'til dawn were long, unbearably long, and they ticked by at a snail's pace. I spent my time digging through the apartment for Agent Wasden's card. I searched high and low, every drawer in the place had been emptied only to find it at long last in my wallet where it had been since the day he first handed it to me.

I showered and readied myself for the day. I was disappointed when I was ready to go at 4:30 a.m. and there was nowhere to go. Agent Wasden was probably as asleep as anyone else I knew at that time of the morning.

When a decent hour rolled around, I made the call and he came. There were local agents, FBI, GBI and the locals, but he came and he stepped on some toes. He turned the entire town on its head, used all of his talents and resources and put the whole CSRA on notice to look for Dwayne Richards, a person of interest in the murder of Wilson Knox. Hometown buy in would get the farthest he thought and left out any mention of Anne at first.

Mr. Watson's initial objective to keep Lucy, Lily and Mrs. Mary from worrying was obliterated. They had to be told what was going on.

When Agent Wasden laid out the details as we knew them, Lucy looked to her father. "You mean Edward's sister and Will were killed because Dwayne Richards is obsessed with me?"

Mr. Watson nodded and there was no stopping the flood of tears that consumed Lucy. Mr. Watson did what everyone in the room wanted to do. He cradled Lucy in his arms and did his level best to assure her that none of this was her fault. In that moment, I realized the weight this knowledge must bear on Lucy and I'd never felt more sorry for anyone in my entire life. I felt somewhat responsible myself, but I could only imagine what this did to her. Wails of pain racked from her as she sobbed and she heaved to catch her breath.

As much as Mr. Watson told her and as much as the rest of us reiterated his words, "Lucy, none of this is your fault," I'm not sure she really heard us. The one thing I was certain of was that it would take her some time to believe it.

Mr. Watson wanted all of us to keep to our normal schedules, but it was hard. Agent Watson agreed that Lucy and I were at the center of whatever Dwayne was up to and we were assigned an entourage of bodyguard types to follow us everywhere.

It was nearly lunchtime when Lucy found me. "Could you help me with Blueberry? I just need him for a minute," Lucy told the Rocky Balboa look alike that was assigned to me.

I dropped what I was doing and went with her. Lucy took my hand and led me down the main corridor of barn.

Lucy had almost avoided me since the night at her house when her father broke the news. My heart hurt waiting for her, but Lily had passed word to me that Lucy just needed some space.

Lucy opened the gate to the stall and showed me in. She'd turned Blueberry out in the paddock and the empty stall confused me. "Lucy?" I was skeptical.

"I've been thinking about it and I want you to join the Navy." Lucy bowed her head and kicked at the fresh straw on the floor of the stall.

"What? Why?" I went to her and she backed up. "I don't understand."

"Oh, Edward, I think we're a toxic mix."

"Are you kidding me? You know that's not true." I couldn't believe what she was saying. I stepped toward to her again. There was nowhere for her to go. She'd backed right into the back wall of the stall.

"Stop." She put her hands out to my chest, but I pushed closer and cornered her.

"I know you love me and you know I love you. I'll join the Navy. I'll do anything you want me to, but not because we are toxic, not because anything that's gone on is our fault. I'll join to make a better life for us in the long run. I'll join to give you a better life than what I can give you now. I'll leave you knowing that I'm always coming back to you, but I won't leave because you're letting some asshole beat us. I won't join to run away."

I lifted her chin to make sure she looked me in the eye. "I've already tried staying away from you because of what he's done and that didn't work. Me without you is not the answer."

"Edward, I can't." The way she leaned into my touch, the heaving of her chest just below the tank top and the flush that reddened her skin, her body gave her away.

"You fought him once, Lucy. Don't give up now." I pressed my nose to hers and caressed the bridge with the tip of mine. I whispered, "Don't give up on us."

Lucy knew what was coming. "I'll scream if you kiss me."

"Then scream."

I licked my lips, moistening them and then pressed mine to hers. It had been at least a week since I'd kissed her. I ached for her as she gave into me. Her hands went to my nape, and I ravaged her mouth. There was no screaming, moans, pleasure, the sweet release of knowing she needed me the way

225

I needed her no matter what she said, but no screaming. The passion between us had to be more than teenage lust. It was love and I'd do anything for her. I meant what I said.

I latched my arms around her thighs and she wrapped her legs around me. Lucy tore at my shirt, pulling at it. All I would have had to do was lift my arms and she'd have stripped me of it. I wanted her, right there and then, and she wanted me. The relief that flooded me, knowing that she still wanted me, fueled the passion I had for her. I resisted the urge to take her in the horse stall. I doubted she would refuse me, but I wouldn't cheapen her by doing that.

One of the straps of her tank top fell as I placed hard kisses from her shoulder down to the top of the blasted thing. Her breast swelled and I slid my tongue in between her cleavage. A breathless cry of, "Oh, Edward," came from her and I could feel the air from her words pass over my ear. Chill bumps ran from my hip down my left leg. No one could do that to me like she could. Chill bumps and a raging hard-on, the ache for her was palpable.

I licked from her cleavage up until I found her mouth again. One more chased kiss and I retreated from her. She fisted my hair and tried to pull me back.

"Not here." I propped my head against hers and tried to regulate my breathing.

"I don't want him to take you too." Lucy squeezed me as if she was holding on for dear life.

"I'm not Anne and I'm not Wilson." I flexed every muscle for her to feel me. "I'll kill him. I'll kill him for you, for Anne, for Wilson. He won't stand a chance."

A glimmer of a smile passed Lucy's lips.

Days passed with no sign of Dwayne. Mr. Evans was questioned and, according to him, the middle of the night comings and goings next door had stopped. Dwayne Richards was in the wind.

To keep interest up with the news stations, Agent Watson flew my mother down and held a press conference with her. He had her tell the story of Anne and a blown up version of Anne's senior picture behind my mother as she spoke. This press conference took place as soon as my mother stepped off of the plane at Bush Field in Augusta, right there on the runway of the airport.

Lucy and I waited to the side as my mother spoke of Anne.

"I can't face her," Lucy clutched my hand.

I didn't know how many times I would have to reassure Lucy that what Dwayne did was not her fault before she started to believe me.

"She's going to love you." I pulled her closer to me and lightly kissed her forehead. "Stop worrying."

My mother began by describing Anne, "This is my baby. I had three and she was the youngest. She loved horses and wanted to be a veterinarian. She was a straight A student and she had the prettiest blue eyes you've ever seen."

The blown up photo of Anne was about a foot behind my mother and to her left. Mother didn't look back, but she reached for the photo and laid an open hand lovingly across Anne's shoulder.

"I'll never kiss her good night again. I'll never see her graduate from high school or college. I'll never help her pick out her wedding dress or see the joy in her eyes after the birth of her children. My baby, my Anne, was stolen from us and all of the joys I would have shared with her were stolen."

My mother held back tears as she spoke, but she continued. "Anne was eighteen and she was at a concert with her brother at his college. He left her for a moment and when he returned she was gone. My baby vanished and no one among forty thousand people saw a thing. It was as if she was never there at all, but she was. She was there and someone took her. Far from her family and deep in some woods along the border between North Carolina and Virginia, he tied her to a tree, stuck what most people know as a Roman Candle, but what the officials termed as a pipe bomb, in her mouth and detonated it. No more blue eyes. No more perfect smile. No more stellar mind. They picked fragments of her skull from the tree tops."

I released Lucy and somewhere during the telling of what had actually happened to my sister, I covered my mouth with both hands.

The final detail my mother imparted was that there wasn't enough of her left by the time Anne's body was found determine if she had been sexually assaulted.

"Now that's something for a mother to take comfort in, right?" Mother sighed and shook her head. "Please help us find who did this to my daughter. We believe this person is operating in your area and is responsible for the death of a local son, Wilson Knox. If you have any details at all," Mother accepted a note card from Agent Wasden and read from it, "Please phone the GBI, the FBI or the local police. The numbers are scrolling at the bottom of your screen. Any and all information is greatly appreciated. Thank you."

Agent Wasden then took the podium and my mother took a stand beside me, opposite Lucy.

"We are in search of a person of interest and hope that the viewing public could help us determine the whereabouts of this individual. Dwayne Richards is a Thomson, Georgia native. He was last seen on July 3, 1997 at approximately 7:00 p.m. in the Thomson area. He drives a late model, red Chevy S-10. He has ruddy reddish brown hair and brown eyes. He is approximately five foot six inches tall and weighs about one hundred and fifty pounds. Mr. Richards is 19 years old. He is missing two fingers on one of his hands. Again, Mr. Richards is wanted for questioning related to the December 7, 1996 abduction and murder of Virginia resident Anne Stephens and the murder of Thomson resident Wilson Knox. As Mrs. Stephens stated, any and all information, no matter how small, is greatly appreciated. Thank you for your time."

I knew now why my mother had kept the details of my sister's death from me. She'd taken special care not to discuss the details with my father while I was around and abiding by her wish was one of the few kindnesses he'd ever done me. She might have refused to allow any of the FBI agents to speak with me about it as well since when I asked they always told me they couldn't divulge information concerning an ongoing investigation, but maybe that's what they told everyone.

Beyond those in horror movies, I'd never seen a mutilated body before, but I had a good idea what one would look like. Where lack of first knowledge left off, my imagination picked up. The images painted in my head of Anne by my mother's description could never been unseen. I had steadied Lucy before, but now with my head spinning and my stomach swirling, she was my rock.

Chapter 21

A fortunate by-product of Wilson Knox's death was hope that my sister's murderer would be caught. Everyone was certain that her murderer and his were one in the same. The effort of every law enforcement agency around single mindedly focused on finding it and proving it.

Dwayne Richards had a very different breed of hounds sniffing him out and he was as elusive as any fox I'd ever tracked. He seemed to be a special kind of sly and lucky. He remained at large for much longer than any of us dreamed.

"How hard could it be to find a three fingered boy in a truck that only half runs on its best day?" Mr. Watson demanded of his former friend, Deputy Harold.

There had been a longstanding open invitation from the hunt to the members of local law enforcement to drop in on Wednesday nights for a free meal. It was one of their ways of thanking them for their service and securing extra patrols around hunt grounds. Deputy Harold mistakenly came out to the hunt club that Wednesday night to partake in the supper that was put on after the hunt.

Heated words such as incompetent and bumbling were aired in Mr. Watson's many grievances against the authorities as to why Dwayne Richards remained at large. Mr. Watson circled the buffet table as Deputy Harold helped himself on the far side. Lucy, Lily, my mother, who was still in town, witnessed the exchange as we ate our dinner from the plates balanced in our laps.

"Please do something," Lucy begged.

"He's gonna slug Daddy and then arrest him." Lily covered her eyes.

I stood to intervene, but I heard my mother's contribution to the conversation. "I guess he can only make an arrest if it's like shooting fish in a barrel."

I stopped in my tracks, turned around and looked at her. What happened to my proper British mother? Reserved and demure, her old qualities, were fading by the day. I waited for my mother to make eye contact with me and I gave her the "be quiet" look.

Mother had postponed her move to England until after Dwayne Richards was captured. She had as much interest in the case as Mr. Watson or any of Wilson Knox's family members, but her newly acquired sharp tongue was not helping.

I defused the situation and the rest of the night was virtually uneventful. Mr. Watson agreed to let me give Lucy a ride home, but I didn't have to take her straight home. While my mother went in the apartment to get ready for bed, Lucy and I took our places on our makeshift front porch.

"Have you heard back from the college about your application?" Lucy asked as she dusted off the spot on the steps next to me.

"No." I sighed, slipping my arm around her.

College and the Navy were two subjects Lucy and I avoided while the hunt was on for Dwayne. Regardless of his capture, the summer would end and a decision had to be made. We both understood that, but neither of us wanted it to be made. It appeared one part of the decision was being made for me. No response from the college was as good as a rejection.

Lucy leaned her head on my shoulder. I could feel her take a couple of deep breaths before she gave her opinion. "I think you should join the Navy."

"Why?" I snatched away and faced her. I couldn't believe we were back to this.

Lucy's eyes glistened. It was more than the moonlight in them. She had tears. "You'll be far from here and far from the reach of Dwayne Richards. I've thought a lot about this and I want you to be safe. You'll be safe in the Navy."

"What about you? I can't leave you. I won't." I reached to pull her into my arms, but she slipped my grasp.

"I've been thinking about this and, for more than one reason, the Navy's the right choice."

"If they don't catch Dwayne by the time school starts, my parents are sending me to the Rabun Gap school. It's a boarding school in Dillard, Georgia."

"What?" I gasped. "But..."

"One of the other attorneys in town sends his daughter there. It's in the mountains and according to my dad it's about as secure as Fort Knox."

"So it doesn't matter if I stay, we still won't be together."

"Right." Lucy bit her lip and shook her head. The moon lit one side of her face and the other was shadowed. "I think we both have to stop living for the here and now and start living for our future. I'm not saying we're done. I just don't think you should wait around here on me. My life isn't my own yet. I'm still at the mercy of my parents and you don't have that obligation."

"Of course we're not done." I wiped away a tear that had escaped her eye.

Lucy smiled. "I wish we could go back to last summer. I know it wasn't drama free, but I miss not being under this microscope."

I inched closer to her and cradled her face in my hands. "I never thought I'd say it, but I miss sneaking around."

Lucy tilted her head as I came in for a kiss. Her hair slipped through my fingers like silk and her tongue tasted like the slice of apple pie we'd just shared for dessert. I hadn't kissed her like that since the last time I'd made love to her and that was before Wilson. I was rock hard and aching for her. It had been weeks and I could have been fine to take her there on the porch if there wasn't a healthy fear of my mother coming out and catching us. The body guards had been let go last week with the belief that Dwayne had left the area so we didn't have to worry about them.

Lucy arched her neck as I planted kisses over her collar bone. "We can sneak around now," she exhaled.

"What do you have in mind?" I breathed the words against her skin in between kisses.

"The stall next to Blueberry's is empty and everyone's gone home for the night."

I raised an eyebrow. Just the thought of having her and I nearly lost myself. "Are you suggesting..."

Lucy rose from her seat on our porch and offered her hand. "No, I'm insisting."

I took her hand and we ran like children down the stairs and through the stables. Just before the stall door I whirled Lucy around and into my arms. "I love you more this year than last, more every day."

I scooped her up and she wrapped herself around me. She cradled my head in her arms and wrapped her legs around my waist. As tiny as she was, Lucy was a force. "I love you more."

I kicked open the stall door and carried her inside. Although I'd had my reservations about cheapening her before, and even now, I wouldn't just have my way with her on the stall floor. I backed her into the corner and pinned her against the wall. The neighing of horses, bucking of hooves on the adjacent stall doors might have been a distraction if I wasn't so completely consumed with desire for her. Every time she told me she loved me made me forget my own name.

"We can take off as much or as little as you like," I offered while unbuttoning her shirt.

Lucy pulled at my collar, starting to lift my shirt over my head. "Take it all off. I don't know when I might see you again and I love looking at you."

I'd always been a bit of an ugly duckling so for anyone to say they enjoyed looking at me was flattering especially when such a statement came from her. If I hadn't been concentrating so hard on getting my shirt over my head while restraining myself from ripping her shirt apart at the seams, I might have blushed.

My logo shirt and undershirt went in one swoop and I was bare-chested. Lucy noticed and licked her lips. If there was a bigger turn on from her, I wasn't sure of it, maybe when she twirled her hair around her finger. I didn't just kiss her then, I devoured her and by some miracle, the buttons on her shirt remained intact. Without breaking our connection, she shimmied out of the shirt and I tossed it to the floor next to my feet.

The lace of Lucy's bra tickled my chest, but didn't distract me from the next chore. "The shorts have got to go."

Lucy giggled. Her laugh was infectious.

Lucy was down to bra and that's it. She helped me get my jeans unbuttoned and then there was no more waiting. They hardly fell before I lifted her and drove in. Lucy screamed a slight startle as I went in. To say it felt good was the greatest of understatements.

"Well, look who I found."

I was so close when the voice came from behind me and shattered the moment. The hair on the back of my neck stood on end and I stilled within her. Lucy's face was over my shoulder and seeing just who it was that interrupted us, she screamed the most blood curdling scream. She jerked back and buried herself in my chest, hiding. The sound of him scared me and the sight of him terrified her. I knew the voice without seeing him. It was my nightmares come to life, Dwayne Richards in proximity to Lucy.

"Let me get my pants," I whispered to her.

I could vaguely make out what she said through her trembling voice, "I think he's got a gun."

"Bend with me and stay behind me." In unison we managed to move in a way to shield her as I pulled up my jeans. I grabbed hers off of the ground while I was down and placed them in her hand. "Take them."

"Whoa there! Did I say you could move?" His voice was as taunting as ever. "Maybe I want to see what everyone else in town's already seen."

I had yet to get a look at him and I figured it wouldn't do any good. He was going to do what he was going to do and I was going to do what I was going to do. I was going to shield Lucy and let her cover herself.

"Oh how I've been waiting to get the two of you alone, especially you, my sweet," Dwayne shuffled in the door way. I could hear his feet rustle on the hay as he shifted sides, trying to get a look at her. I was so very grateful for her petite frame. She was small enough that I completely concealed her. I'd die before he got a look at her, making some sort of sick memory to use for his pleasure.

For a second, I thought of my mother being right above us in my apartment. Maybe she'd heard Lucy scream. I didn't know if that was a good or bad thing. Maybe Mother would be safe if she stayed upstairs or maybe if she came down she could somehow help us. I squinted my eyes and pushed the what-ifs and maybes away. All I had to count on was the here and now and right then I had to focus on protecting Lucy. I had to figure out a way to get us out of this, a way to kill Dwayne Richards. We were cornered in the stall so flight wasn't an option. I knew I had to fight.

"I said get out of the way!" Dwayne growled.

The button on my jeans was done and Lucy was stepping into her shorts. Although I still lacked my shirt and so did Lucy, we were close to being decent. I was close to being in a position to face him.

"Whatever you have planned for us, you can do with us clothed," I barked back at him.

"Ever the big man, Eddie. Well, I've got something for that." That's when I heard the hammer of the gun, that unmistakable cocking noise.

"Oh, God, Edward!" Lucy slid around me so quickly I hardly had time to grab her and keep her from putting herself between us. She would have taken a bullet for me.

"Lucy, no!" I shoved her behind me again. Before I really knew what I was saying that classic saying came out, "Why don't you pick on..."

Dwayne cut me off. "I already did. I picked on your sister." He glared at me.

I bowed my chest. He wasn't my size. He was barely taller than Lucy. Without that pistol, he'd be no match for me. I hardly saw the gun. All I saw was rage and all I felt was the need to avenge my sister. I was blinded by the need to snap his neck or rip his little ice cube of a heart out with my bare hands.

I would have charged at him, regardless of the gun, and given him what he wanted. I would have given him the opportunity to kill me on the spot. I would have too, if Lucy hadn't dug her nails into my back. She meant to get my attention and she did. The pain of her nails cutting through me reminded me I had more at stake than just getting revenge. I had to protect her.

"Settle down there, Eddie. I realize I didn't let you finish, but don't take out your frustrations on me." Every word he said put an image in my head that aimed to infuriate me. He knew exactly what he was doing, but apparently so did Lucy.

Lucy withdrew her claws and while appearing to hide her face behind me she blew over the marks she'd just left in my back. The image of her face, whisps of her hair framing it, replaced the dark images Dwayne was planting. Focusing on her would get us out of here. Thinking clearly and rationally, using my mind, that's what would get us out of this. I had to out think him.

"So Lucy, I see you made it out of the woods that day."

I reached back and clasped her hand in mine. "And we see you made it out of exile."

"What are you doing?" Lucy whispered in a voice I could hardly hear for Dwayne's shouting.

"I wasn't talking to you!" He waived the gun at me.

"Really? I totally forgot that you only pick on women and young boys. Forgive me." I smirked. Maybe taunting him back would get him to do something stupid. After all, he didn't have Lucy holding him back.

"So, how's your sister?" He shifted again, back and forth, still blocking the gate leading out of the stall.

"Which one?" I raised an eyebrow and challenged him.

Dwayne smiled. He was in dire need of a dentist. Plaque filled each grove between his upper teeth. He'd let himself go or perhaps he was always this nasty and I'd never paid any attention before.

"So what do you plan to do to us? I mean, we need to get moving."

"Aren't you a breath of fresh air? Everyone else has begged and begged for me to let them go, not for me to get it over with."

"Lucy here's got a curfew and if I don't have her home everyone in town will be looking for her."

"I guess that would be a nice change from them looking for me." Another smile.

I smiled back, but I wanted to vomit. I wanted to punch that grin off of his face and vomit. I kept my cool and prodded again. "Well, what's the plan?"

"You'll know soon enough." Dwayne backed up from the door way and motion us out with the barrel of the gun.

"Can you give us a second?" I asked politely before telling Lucy over my shoulder, "Get your shirt."

Lucy was still braced against my back. I could feel her, too terrified to move more than her involuntary shaking.

"It's okay, Lucy, he's not going to hurt us here. Get your shirt." Dwayne turned up his nose as I made my assurances.

Inching over to where I had tossed the shirt, I moved with her so she remained safely behind me.

Once she was completely covered, Dwayne motioned impatiently with the gun. "Get moving!"

I didn't know what I was going to do to save us, but I knew I had to do something. It had to happen soon. We didn't stand a chance in the confines of the stall, but both Lucy and I were in our element in the hunt barn. If we were going to stand a chance against him, it would have to be while we were still at the barn.

Dwayne hung behind and insisted that I go ahead. I started to maneuver Lucy in front of me, again trying to shield her from him, but he stopped her. I glanced back to see him sizing her up.

"It will be hard, but I'll forgive you for this." He salivated over her and ran that mangled hand of his up her arm. "We all do things we shouldn't."

The look on her face was pure repulsion. She drew her arm up close to her body. I was scared she was going to tell him to go to Hell or worse. She didn't. She pursed her lips and turned up her nose.

I thought about making a play for the gun while Dwayne was distracted with Lucy, but their moment didn't last long enough.

"Let's get moving. I have to get rid of the competition." He poked me with the gun and gave me a shove.

It appeared he was leading us to the far end of the barn, toward the parking lot. We were coming up on the midway point, where the barn opened in the center and led out the front. If I distracted Dwayne, Lucy could run out the front of the barn. She could run upstairs to the apartment, warn my mother and they could call the police or she could just run out front and hide in one of the other stables out there.

I made my mind up and when we got even with the opening, I pretended to trip. Dwayne was close behind me and I did it quick enough that he couldn't stop before tripping with me.

"Run, Lucy!" I shoved her toward the corridor leading out front as I went down.

Everything happened so fast. There was a flash and a nose that rang my ears and deafened me to all other sounds. I was flat on the floor of the thoroughfare through the stable. Regaining my senses, I saw Dwayne standing over me, pointing the gun. It was smoking. Had he shot me? I wasn't in any pain. I couldn't hear, but other than the racing of my heart, I felt okay. Panicked as I looked around for Lucy, but I think I was alright.

"Get up!" I could tell by the strain on his face that he was screaming at me, but I barely heard him above a whisper. He frantically looked from left to right. He was shouting, "LUCY!"

I looked around as well, but I didn't see Lucy anywhere. I hoped she got away. She'd ran down the corridor to the front like I'd intended. I hope she ran upstairs and was calling the police.

Dwayne kept stomping about, screaming, waiving the gun and then pointing it at me. My ears were ringing. Evidently he'd landed a shot very near my head. I didn't care. I took comfort in Lucy having run away. If he shot me now, at least I'd given her a chance.

My hearing was starting to return. The strain on his face and in his neck let me know he was still shouting, but the words came through as a frantic whisper.

"I'm so going to kill you! Even if I have to come back for her later. You're going to be the grand finale at the Independence day celebration, my independence. You are going to die, Eddie!"

Chapter 22

Dear Lucy,

I know you said you needed some time, but I am going to continue to write to you. You may not recall, but this is the anniversary of Anne's disappearance. It was not my call to you that started all of this. It was my failure to call you. I should have called you all along. I should have pursued you from the moment I met you. Like you are doing now, I tried to lock away my heart to protect you and to protect myself. As you feel now, I felt then. There were so many reasons that I should have let you go, but I couldn't. I pray that you will take your time and realize that you cannot let me go. If I had listened to my heart from the beginning, I would have never felt the pull to leave Anne alone that night and call you when I did.

Tonight I am writing to you from somewhere in the Gulf of Arden. The Gulf of Arden is at the southern end of the Red Sea and feeds into the Arabian Sea. The night is clear and there are more stars than I could count in a lifetime. Looking up at them reminds me of sitting on our makeshift porch outside of the apartment at the hunt barn. It's just as beautiful, but isn't nearly the same because you are not sitting here looking up at them with me.

I am on board a small ship that escorts an aircraft carrier and this will be my home for the foreseeable future. I boarded the ship while it was docked for refueling in Yemen. Yemen is tense. We were warned early on that Americans are not their favorite people there. Other than that things are going well.

As you know from my letters, basic training wasn't hard. The days were long, but it wasn't nearly as bad as I thought it was going to be. I think looking at your picture made things easier for me. Knowing that Dwayne Richards could never hurt you or anyone else ever again made things bearable as well. I know we don't see eye to eye on the subject of how things ended with Dwayne, but I understand and respect your point of view. I just wanted you to know that.

I have spoken with the ship chaplain about what went on and he told me that it must be a heavy burden to know that someone loved you enough to kill for you. Seeing me kill Dwayne, even though in self-defense, and his blood literally on my hands, must have been hard on you and a memory that you cannot shake. I have visited with the chaplain regularly since I arrived. What I did has been a burden for me as well, but I cannot tell you I would change a thing. Protecting you from him was an easy choice and it always will be, but that doesn't make me heartless to the fact that I killed someone. Killing him with my bare hands is not a memory I like to relive, but I did what I had to do. I will forever feel the guilt of leaving my sister at the concert that night last year, but I'll never live with the guilt of avenging her or protecting you. I know it is hard for you to look at me without seeing Dwayne's blood, but one day, when this is not so

*fresh in your mind, I hope you will understand why
I did what I did.*

*From my seat here on the deck I can see the
Big Dipper. I can't help but hope you are looking at
the same sky and thinking of me. Ultimately, I
know that's not possible because it is daylight where
you are, but I am holding out hope anyway. Mostly,
I hope you're missing me as much I'm missing you,
but that's not my greatest hope. My greatest hope is
that you will be happy. With or without me, I hope
you will have a happy life.*

*I know things are busy for you with starting
your senior year of high school at a new school, but
I hope you find the time to write me back. I will
continue to write to you at least once a week, but
please do not feel pressured to write me back as
often. I believe your focus should be on school and I
understand if it is. Please know that as far away as
I am, I am still here for you. I am still yours. I will
always be yours.*

> *Love always,*
> *Your Edward*

I signed the letter, then I folded and sealed it
in the envelope I'd addressed to Lucy at the Rabun
Gap Nacoochee School. Her parents decided to spare
her having to face the kids of Thomson High with the
whole town knowing what happened to Dwayne
Richards and Wilson Knox. They felt prying eyes,
gossip and continual questions about a boy that
killed two people over his obsession with her would
only cause her more grief. If ever anyone had
suffered enough at such a young age, it was Lucy

Meeks. Lucy agreed with her parents' decision and went willingly.

I'd finished the letter to Lucy, but as I sat on the deck of the ship, I looked out over the sparkling horizon. Along with the stars in the sky and their reflections on the waves, I could see the lights of the carrier in the distance. The night unfolded before me and I thought of Lucy.

The Navy was a way of furthering my education, building a future for Lucy and me, and passing the time until we could be together. It wasn't a fresh start for me, but I feared Lucy was seizing the opportunity for a fresh start by leaving Thomson. From the moment she pulled me off of Dwayne Richards unrecognizable body, she'd never looked at me the same.

To this day, I'm not sure how I bested him. There was a noise, Blueberry going nuts bucking the stall and the other horses spooked by the screaming and gun shots or something from down in the direction Lucy had ran when I shoved her. As I was regaining my bearings, he glanced that way for just a split second. He still had the gun trained on me, but I caught him off guard and swept his legs out from under him. The gun went off again and for the second time I somehow dodged a bullet. I was nearly deaf from the first round and the second firing didn't help my hearing, but that didn't stop me and it didn't even slow me down.

When Dwayne's feet went out from under him he lost the grip on the gun and it flew out of his hand. There was no time for him to try to grab it as he hit the ground and I scrambled on top of him. I caught him completely off guard. He hardly put up a fight, a couple of blows and he cowered with his fists round his head, trying to protect himself. I gave him a couple of jabs to the ribs and he uncovered his face. I'm not sure how many times I hit him. I just went for it as hard as I could blow after blow.

My mother and Lucy had heard the second shot and as my mother finished the call to the police for help, Lucy came running back for me. Lucy found me still beating Dwayne about the face. She said she called my name, but I didn't hear her. She pulled me off of him and saw his face. She later described a grotesque scene of blood with a concave blob of red with only hints of crushed bone protruding. From the damage done to my hands, broken fingers and busted knuckles, I believed Lucy. I'd punched him in the face until there was nothing left of him. The really terrible part of it is that as hard as I tried to remember what he looked like, what I did to him, I couldn't. It really was a blur from the first blow to Lucy pulling me off of him. When she pulled me off, my eyes trained on her. I was so relieved she'd gotten away and that we were safe that I couldn't think of anything else. My mind went blank and I don't remember hardly anything from the rest of the night. I remember her holding me and me holding her. That was all that mattered to me.

A million moments with Lucy played out in my head. Good memories, bad memories, they rolled from one to the next like a movie. I would have given anything to transport back in time to the moment I met her and start over again. If I could get back to the beginning, maybe I could save us all.

247

***

It was Christmas morning 1997 on the east coast of the United States, but in the middle of the Agean Sea, it was just after 5:00 p.m., well into Christmas Day. A ship to shore call was our Christmas present from the Navy. Each seaman was allowed one. I was lucky to have drawn a shift that allowed me to call home, Lucy's home, at a decent hour.

The days that Lucy and I spent finishing out the summer were not the most pleasant. We weren't at each other's throats. It would have been better if we were. Then maybe it wouldn't have come as such a shock when she completely backed away the last week we were to spend together before she left for boarding school and I'd left for basic training.

"I think we should take this time apart to work on ourselves," Lucy said.

I remember it clearly. We were sitting in the swing on the front porch of the Watson house. It was Sunday and I'd been invited over by Mr. Watson for Sunday lunch. There was a slight breeze and Lucy's hair was blowing in it. I reached to take her hand and she pulled away. The translation wasn't necessary. I felt a dark cloud hovering over us and I knew what the cloud was. I just didn't know how the cloud would affect us. Lucy proposed we see the coming time apart as a time of reflection, a break, but not a breakup.

Although I'd written to Lucy once per week since I'd left for basic, she'd rarely written back. I feared the break really was a breakup. The more the phone rang before being answered, the more I felt the distance wasn't just in mileage.

Finally, Lily picked up. "Merry Christmas!"

I responded in kind.

"Oh, Edward! Let me get Lucy!" There was more excitement in Lily's voice than one would expect in a typical greeting. Before I could thank her, she was yelling Lucy's name. I heard a muffled version as she likely put her hand over the phone.

"Hey." Lucy wasn't nearly as excited as Lily was and I tried not to read too much into it.

"Hey," I replied. "Merry Christmas."

"I miss you."

The words hung in the air and I could hardly breathe. I'd wanted to hear her voice and hear her say those words for so long. I didn't know what to say. I wanted to thank her because as long as she missed me I felt I there was still a chance for us.

"Are you still there?"

"Yeah. I miss you, too."

"I wish you were here."

"Me, too."

"I'm sorry I haven't written much."

"I'm sorry if I've written too much."

"Don't be. I love getting your letters. I look forward to them."

My heart was beating out of my chest. I slinked back against the wall next to the phone. There was no privacy due to the line of sailors behind me waiting to use the phone, but for all I cared, I might as well have been in a phone booth. I closed my eyes and all I saw was Lucy's face. Her eyes smiled and danced just for me. This was my real Christmas present.

I guess I was too quiet again so Lucy picked the conversation again. "Edward, I don't know if I ever told you, but I'm proud of you."

"For what?"

"For saving us. For taking my father's advice and joining the Navy. For taking a chance on us having a future and most of all for being you."

"Lucy..."

"Yes, Edward?"

"I'm going to marry you one day."

"I know."

The end...for now.

Dear Readers,

As always, thank you so much for giving your time to my writing. I hope you have enjoyed this book.

I am currently working on my next book, "My Summer With the Senator", which will begin a new series.

I aim to follow-up with that book and then return to The Wrightsboro Hunt. If you enjoyed Lucy and Edward's story please check out my other books while you wait for what is in store for Lucy, Edward, Lily, Mr. Watson and the rest of the members of the hunt.

Your feedback is always appreciated and I love hearing from you. Please feel free to leave me reviews on Amazon.com as those are invaluable to authors, follow me on Facebook at my author page, T.S. Dawson Author, or email me directly through the contact section of my website (TSDawson.com).

Words cannot convey the appreciation I feel for your interest in my books. All I can say is thank you.

Sincerely,

T.S. Dawson
And the Entire T.S. Dawson team

Other T.S. Dawson books available on Amazon:

Port Honor (The Honor Series)

In Search of Honor (2nd in the series)

The Price of Honor (3rd in the series)

When I Was Green (Wrightsboro Hunt Series)

www.ingramcontent.com/pod-product-compliance
Lightning Source LLC
Chambersburg PA
CBHW071142170626
46809CB00002B/740